Something from Below

Something from Below

S. T. Joshi

Hippocampus Press

New York

Published by Hippocampus Press
P.O. Box 641, New York, NY 10156.
www.hippocampuspress.com

First published by PS Publishing, 2019.

Hippocampus Press logo designed by Anastasia Damianakos.

First Hippocampus Press edition, 2021
1 3 5 7 9 8 6 4 2

ISBN 978-1-61498-323-1

Something from Below

1

I can't tell you why exactly I returned to Dunsmuir after I graduated from Lehigh. It had something to do with my mother, who had wrapped herself in a cloak of studied helplessness after my father died during my junior year. The funny thing is that Mom—and Dad too, even if his inveterate taciturnity had prevented him from articulating it—were determined that I leave my hometown for good and go somewhere else, *anywhere* else, to seek my fortune and my happiness. Maybe Mom thought my return would only be temporary, and I for one was fervently hoping the same thing. After what's happened, I really don't know what I want to do. I'm as terrified of leaving as I am of staying.

I have to admit that my return also had something to do with Randy. But I'll get into that later.

I trudged up to my front door (but was it really "my" front door anymore?), leaving my few belongings in my used Mini Cooper, where they fit easily with room to spare. I felt funny knocking on the door—the door I'd gone in and out of an incalculable number of times in the first eighteen years of my life—but I'd lost or misplaced the key to the house and couldn't bother looking for it.

My mother opened the door after what seemed like an eternity.

"Hi, Alison," she said unenthusiastically.

"Hi, Mom," I said.

My mother had, in the year and half since my father had died, gained a kind of resentful and put-upon expression, as if irked at the thought of having to carry the weight of the world—and its multifarious annoyances, tragedies, and heart-breaks—on her shoulders but knowing that no one else had the wherewithal to do so. She had never been cheerful, but now her wisps of unruly salt-and-pepper hair, the creases in her face, the slumped shoulders, and (I'm sorry to have to say it) the general lumpishness of her figure made her seem a full two decades older than her forty-five years. It was hard for me to remember that, when I was a little girl, I once thought her the most beautiful woman I'd ever seen.

We hugged tentatively and formulaically, and I walked in. Not one thing seemed to have changed since my last visit. This tiny house—one story and unfinished basement—was exactly the sort of place you'd expect a (now deceased) coal miner and his much-suffering wife to own. Built in the 1940s to house the GI's returning from the war so that they could once again take their accustomed place in the underground labyrinths of the Brashear mine, it seemed more like a barracks than a home. Since I'd known nothing else when growing up, I'd paid no attention to its dinginess, the tiny rooms that barely accommodated the cheap sticks of furniture we had, and the few and meager plants that my mother once—but no more—took the trouble to plant in the front yard.

To me, this was still *home*—and the strange and horrible thing was that it still tugged at my heart in a way that made me wonder if, no matter how long I lived and where else I lay down to sleep at night, any other place would ever be home in quite the same way.

But I wasn't the same person I was when I left for college

four years ago. My mind had expanded—I proudly sported a degree in chemistry, although in my unworldliness I hadn't the faintest idea what kind of gainful employment I could find with it—and my understanding of the world had expanded too, exponentially so. That point had been hammered home to me in no uncertain terms when I missed my father's funeral.

I had been spending the first semester of my junior year in France—pursuing an even more impractical minor in art history—when the dreadful news had come. And yet, my mother had magnanimously advised me not to bother coming home ("It's such a long way, and there's really nothing you can do"). I had a feeling that what she really meant was that she didn't have the funds to pay for a hastily arranged international flight, and I certainly didn't. She had reacted to my dad's death with a kind of resigned equanimity—as if his more than two decades in working in the Brashear mine were in themselves a kind of slow-acting death sentence. And maybe they were.

If I was surprised at my mother's apparent indifference to the death of her husband of twenty-two years, I was even more surprised at a certain sequel that removed the fear that I'd have to come home anyway because my family—now reduced to my mother and some distant aunts, uncles, and cousins with whom we had little to do—could no longer afford to keep me in college, in spite of the likelihood that Lehigh would augment my financial aid because the breadwinner in my household was suddenly taken from us. What happened was that Conrad Brashear, the current owner of the mine that had been in his family for generations, had generously granted my mother a modest stipend that would endure for the rest of her life, and also assured her that my remaining college expenses (only for undergraduate work, it was blandly explained) would also be taken care of.

Was this some kind of veiled admission of culpability on Brashear's part? It did not appear so; for he seems to have acted similarly in numerous other instances of miners' deaths or injuries, few of which could be laid to negligence or chicanery on his part. My increasingly liberal political views left me unprepared for this striking instance of benevolent plutocracy. Maybe, I said to myself, I'd have to give Mr. Brashear my thanks in person—assuming I was allowed entrance into his surprisingly modest mini-mansion on the north part of town.

If you haven't heard of Dunsmuir, you're not alone. It's tucked away in a remote corner of northeastern Pennsylvania, not far from the Delaware River and the border with New York State. It is so far to the east of I-81—which bisects eastern Pennsylvania from north to south—that there's not even a sign for it on the Interstate. I can't be bothered to tell you how many state and county roads you need to get there. There's no reason why anyone except those who live here would ever want to come.

The descendants of the Scotch-Irish worthies who had founded the town in the late eighteenth century had mostly gone on to more prosperous zones—Allentown, Bethlehem, even what has now become the megalopolis of Philadelphia. Curiously, my own line, the Mannerings, had remained; my father's parents, a little too devoted to Sir Walter Scott, had named their son Guy, but at the same time had made it clear that his only feasible employment would be the mine. That mine remained the largest employer in Dunsmuir—a town whose population barely exceeded 1000 and was not likely to grow anytime soon.

If you don't know any other place else, even the most dismal locale can have the comfort and security of home. I can't complain about my childhood: my parents did all they could to shield me from the harshness of life as a coal miner's daughter, and I had my share of friends at the small elementary school and even smaller high school in town. No one—except Conrad Brashear and a few other bigwigs—were living high on the hog, and we kids (and parents too, for that matter) just got used to making do with a little. I never had an allowance, we rarely went to any fancy places on vacations (a trip to the Delaware Water Gap was considered a luxurious treat), and all summer we were left to play among ourselves rather than trooping off to some expensive and exclusive camp. But that was fine with us; with our limited resources we exercised our imaginations to come up with our own sports and games, and I can't honestly say I felt "deprived" in any meaningful way.

In a sense, going off to Lehigh was a mistake—or, at least, it had the effect of making me realize how small and unprivileged my upbringing was. That college had its share of high-born preppies, and they made it abundantly clear that I wasn't even to dream of being part of their circle. Well, that was fine with me—but the drawback was that, now that I had come home, "home" itself didn't seem such a nice place anymore. My horizons having widened, I resented even a temporary return to the narrow, confining world of Dunsmuir.

I had arrived early in the afternoon on that day in late May, and it took little time to dump my few belongings into my old room (yes, it inevitably seemed a lot smaller than I had remembered it even from four years ago) or in the basement for future disposal. Mom didn't lift a finger to help, but that was all right. What she did do was peer at me with an inscrutable expression on her face, as if I were some kind of hallucination that would dissipate if she kept staring long enough. Her features had gained a cast of perpetual melancholy, and now they were fused with a welter of other thoughts and feelings. *You really shouldn't be here . . . Why did you come back? . . . I love having you here, but you're not really my little girl anymore, are you? . . . I think something bad is going to happen now that you're here . . .*

She articulated none of these thoughts, but said a bit mechanically: "Are you hungry? I can make you some lunch."

"Never mind, Mom," I said, dumping a duffel bag full of books on the living room floor, unable to carry it all the way into my bedroom. "I had something on the road."

She nodded absently, as if she really hadn't wanted to make lunch for me but felt duty-bound to offer. Cooking was, in fact, one of her few creative outlets, and she took justifiable pride in making tasty meals out of whatever foodstuffs her tight budget allowed. She must have been frustrated in the past year and a half with no one to cook for: cooking for one is no fun. No doubt she would reserve her culinary skills for dinner, and I suspected I would have to justify my presence here by eating it appreciatively.

As I've said, I didn't have a lot of stuff to bring into the house, but even this modest amount—following the nearly three-hour drive from Lehigh—proved exhausting. I sat down heavily on the ancient couch in the living room, taking a strange comfort in its frayed upholstery and lumpy cushions. Mom initially fluttered nervously around me, already unused to having another person in the house after eighteen months of solitude; then, realizing that it was long past the time when she should be a helicopter parent, she sat down demurely next to me.

She began to speak in a high, flutey kind of voice that I didn't recall her using before. "So what are you going to—?"

But I interrupted her. "I'd like to see Daddy's grave."

It was obviously not what she was expecting to hear. Her

mouth closed with an audible click of her teeth, and she gazed at me as if I had asked her to board a spaceship to Mars.

"Why . . . ?" she began.

"Mom," I said impatiently, "he's my dad, and he's dead! Don't you think I want to see where he's buried?"

"Of course you do, dear," she said patronizingly, looking away from me.

"Well, can you take me?" I said, more heatedly than I probably should have. I wasn't even sure why I was asking: there was only one cemetery in town, and no doubt I could have figured out my dad's burial plot after a certain amount of hunting. But my mom's curious hesitancy on the matter puzzled and hurt me.

"Right now?" she said feebly, hoping against hope that maybe I really meant I wanted to go tomorrow, or next week, or next year.

"Yes, right now," I said, looking right at her.

This was perhaps the first tiny instance of a shift in our relationship—the first indication that I wasn't someone she could bully and subdue merely by virtue of being older and being my parent. True, she had never been a bully; if I thought of her as such, it was only because she had to fill the role of disciplinarian after it became abundantly clear that Daddy was only interested in being my indulgent pal and comrade, willing to accommodate my every wish (within reason, of course—and within our limited means) and even interfering ineffectually when my mother sought to punish me for my various derelictions. There was, mercifully, no indication on Daddy's part that he had wished I was a boy; in fact, he seemed more tickled than Mom was at my being female, and it was only recently that I began to understand why.

I, at least, wouldn't be working in the Brashear mine.

Mom lifted herself up heavily from the couch, an aggrieved expression on her face. It was as if she was saying: *Not only is the weight of the world on my shoulders, but now I have to deal with a suddenly rebellious daughter.* Even though it was warm, she made a pointed effort to look for an appropriate wrap to brave the non-existent elements, finally deciding upon a dark blue cardigan that evoked deep memories in me—trips to the one playground in town, where Mom would look apprehensively at me as I ventured with increasing boldness on the swing and monkey bars; the almost daily shopping trips to the discount grocery, where she weighed the relative cost of different brands with the keen-eyed precision of a gem dealer; and visits in our rattletrap Oldsmobile to her relatives in nearby Fenton, with my father pointedly absent, since her side of the family regarded the union as a social and financial catastrophe.

I bundled her into my Mini and drove off. I hadn't lived in town for four years, but I knew the way.

The cemetery—a non-denominational one that labored under the tiresome euphemism Shady Haven—was on the western edge of town, as if the grim reality of death could somehow be disregarded by mere physical distance. It took minutes to drive there, but once I'd pulled into the long entryway I had to appeal silently to Mom to lead us to the plot. What few relations I had on either side of the family were buried elsewhere, and I couldn't recall attending a single funeral in my childhood or adolescence. Both sets of grandparents were still in the land of the living and not at all old—but I did wonder if a rash of interments might suddenly follow in the coming years.

Mom grudgingly indicated a road that led off to the left of the main drive, and I followed it, driving at a respectfully slow pace even though not a soul seemed to be present, either in a car or on foot.

After taking a right off of this road, I was startled by Mom's abrupt comment: "Right here."

I didn't see Dad's name on any of the tombstones facing the road on the right, where Mom had fractionally bent her head as she had said those two laconic words. As I stopped the car and got out, I was irked that she didn't follow suit. I raised my eyebrows, then frowned, but still she remained mulishly immobile.

I had no choice but to stalk around the front of the car and open the passenger-side door. "Can you show me?" I said with more than a little irritation in my voice.

She sighed as if I were making some outrageously irrational request, but did make a move—but only after several seconds, in one last futile gesture of defiance.

We trudged off through the grass to our right, making sure not to step on any headstones lying flat on the ground. Within minutes we reached the spot.

I'm not sure what I was expecting to feel when I saw the simple marker ("GUY MANNERING / 1970–2016"), but for reasons I couldn't quite understand I got so choked up that I had to suppress a gasping cry. I placed my hand over my mouth, and my eyes filled with tears. I couldn't remember the last time I had cried—I'm not a "girly girl" in that respect—but I came close to it then.

In a fleeting moment of tenderness and solidarity, Mom rubbed my back and shoulders, her face almost crumpling in sympathetic grief and agony. But she said nothing.

I got hold of my emotions enough to say, "How did he die?"

The question might have seemed strange under any other circumstances—but the fact of the matter is that Mom had failed to explain the exact cause and manner of Dad's death in that absurdly short phone call she had made to me while I was in France. I had asked her at the time myself, seeking to digest the stunning news, but she had claimed that the cost of the phone call was so exorbitant that there was no point going into the matter. It would be unfair of me to say that she was calm and undisturbed during that awful phone call; but somehow I got the impression that, for her, death was a not entirely unexpected occupational hazard at a mine, and that it just happened to be Daddy's turn to fall victim to it.

And, in spite of my shock and horror at the time, there was some deep part of me that agreed with her.

But I needed some more explanation now. Exactly why, I couldn't have articulated even to myself. The contemptible buzzword "closure" has nothing to do with it: Daddy was dead, and there was nothing more to be done about it. And it certainly wasn't the case that I wanted confirmation that coal mining was a dirty and dangerous business—I knew that already.

Mom, taken aback at my question, reacted with weak bluster. "He died in the mine, of course."

"I know that, Mom—you told me. But how, exactly?"

It was then that something odd happened. I wouldn't have been surprised if she had been angry or pained or outraged. After all, she was the one who had been on the scene when it had happened—and she, as a wife, might in some perverse way have felt more entitled to supremacy in grief than a daughter. She claimed not to have held it against me that I had not come back for the funeral, but perhaps there was a latent resentment there, unspoken but festering in her heart.

But no—she expressed none of these emotions. As she remained silent, looking at me wide-eyed, I had to make a clumsy guess at what she was feeling.

And what she seemed to be feeling was . . . fear.

It was absurd, of course: men died in mines all the time.

From coal dust, from a cave-in, from all manner of other threats that constantly hemmed them in as they tunneled like huge moles into the bowels of the earth. So what was the big deal about telling me? Did Mom think I was some sort of "delicate lass" who couldn't endure a plain account of my father's mortality? Did she, in some horrible way, feel that a full explanation would cause my grief to be equated with hers?

If she had only told me the full truth then, a lot of pain and horror could have been avoided. But the fundamental horror would still have remained.

"He just died," Mom said, scowling and looking away from me. "I don't know the details."

"You don't *know?*" I said incredulously. "How is that possible?"

"Well," she almost wailed, "it wasn't as if I was there! They just brought his body to the morgue, and I never even saw it. There was a closed-casket service."

I struggled to digest it all. Could Dad's body have been crushed somehow? I had not heard of any such incident—but perhaps I wouldn't have, being a continent away when it had happened. Mom was never much for writing letters, and I don't believe she wrote me a single letter when I was in France. Dad had written a few pathetically illiterate notes before his death, but after his passing Mom was stonily silent, and I myself stopped writing to her. My resentment against her had been such that I had refused to come home that summer—the summer after my junior year—and that hadn't helped in re-establishing mother-daughter intimacy after Dad was gone.

I marched away from the plot in disgust, now wanting to get as far away from it as possible. My daddy really wasn't there, I said to myself sulkily—not the daddy who had meant so much to me. His corpse—perhaps mutilated beyond recognition, and beyond the reparations of the most skilled mortician—may have been submerged there under that bland headstone, but he would now live only in my memories.

Mom trudged after me: she now seemed the recalcitrant child, I the imperious parent. We got back into the car and drove off.

As if to make amends, Mom expended more than her usual considerable effort in preparing a tasty dinner for me—roast chicken, fresh-made biscuits, sautéed green beans, and peach cobbler for dessert. I ate as much of it as I could, but it all tasted like ashes in my mouth. I was gratified by her exertions, but felt that they were a kind of smokescreen that was designed to preclude the possibility of further investigation by the sheer weight of calories, fat, meat, and sugar. And it worked: we said little as we shoveled forkful after forkful of the stuff into our mouths.

After dinner, I said I needed to go out, and she didn't stop me. She knew I was going to see Randy.

2

Randy Kroeber first came to my attention around sophomore year in high school. At first he seemed sadly representative of the stultified, backwoods population of Dunsmuir—a population that readily allows people of more privileged backgrounds to look down on us as rednecks or patronize us with the demeaning epithet "working class." His father was a coal miner and he was destined to end up there himself: the idea of going to college would have been as remote from his mind as becoming a Buddhist monk and moving to Tibet. He was tall, lanky, with a shock of unruly black hair that framed a long face with angular features that few would have considered attractive; but there was something in his brooding countenance and shuffling walk that paradoxically appealed to me, if only because I had so much trouble figuring out how he could so limit his horizons. He seemed wearily content to follow the path that had been set for him almost since his birth, and the idea of rebelling against it was beyond the powers of his imagination.

But it was during junior year that he and I became close— and more than close. We were in the same English class—for the high school, in its infinite wisdom, decreed that students must pass three years of English and three years of math to graduate—and it quickly became obvious to me that he was struggling. I have to confess that it was largely pity that led me to offer my help: seeing someone suffer so acutely at what to me was so effortless (in spite of my heavy preference for the sciences over the humanities) caused me such pain that I felt the need to alleviate it, just to make myself feel better.

We were supposed to write a "critical analysis"—in other words, a glorified book report—on a book of our choice, to be picked from a list of a dozen titles the teacher, Mr. Kratzner, offered. You can imagine what was on the list—*The Catcher in the Rye, The Pearl, Johnny Got His Gun,* and so on. Randy chose Steinbeck's *Of Mice and Men*—probably because it was one of the shortest.

But with even this simple tale of shattered dreams and mind-numbing trauma he had difficulty. He just couldn't get it through his head how an "analysis" of a made-up story written by a man long dead could be of any value or relevance to his life—and, in all honesty, I had to agree he had a point. But it was an assignment, and nothing he could say or do would get him out of it.

So he began coming over to our house, plodding along with his bag of books and other paraphernalia as if it was one of the "fardels" that Shakespeare says we all must bear. I had already read the book, even though I was writing on another one (Dostoevsky's *Crime and Punishment*), so I offered what help I could.

He would sit on the floor, pawing through the slim paperback copy with a kind of frustrated hatred. He had in fact been diligent in reading the text, but its "tragic" ending—and, in general, the generally lugubrious tone of the whole work—had affected him more than he was willing to let on.

But trying to articulate his feelings about the book—which, in fact, was all that Mr. Kratzner really wanted or had any right to expect of his largely "working-class" pupils—was nearly beyond Randy's abilities.

I wanted to help him, but drew the line at actually writing his paper for him, as Randy had initially suggested.

"Come on, Randy," I said, losing my patience a bit at what struck me as his almost willful refusal to think for himself, "you can do this."

He just shook his head disconsolately.

"It's not as hard as you're making it out to be," I said, trying to be reassuring.

He eyed me sourly, but said nothing.

"What about Lennie?" I said in a kind of desperation. "Lennie's really the heart of the book, don't you think?"

Randy's mouth twisted in an uncharacteristic sneer. "He's a stupid fool," he said scornfully.

"Randy," I said tartly, "Lennie's not stupid. He has mental problems, but his heart is in the right place, don't you think?"

"Why does he kill everything he touches?" Randy almost whined.

"Sometimes you kill the things you love, don't you, Randy?"

I have no idea why I said that. We were all of sixteen, and I don't suppose either of us knew very much about love beyond what we saw on the contrived TV shows we were all addicted to. But my comment seemed to sink in, for Randy looked down at his own hands as if they were Lennie's, stroking a rabbit or a puppy until he inadvertently twisted its neck.

Let me say right here that Randy himself wasn't at all stupid: I certainly didn't think of him as some hideous parallel to Steinbeck's Lennie Small. He had a lot of native intelligence—it just wasn't the book-learning that so many schools want. I was a bit surprised Randy was even still in school, for a certain number of his compatriots had already dropped out, knowing they'd spend their lives underground and figuring they might as well waste no time getting there.

But what Randy did at that moment surprised me—no, shocked me. He began to cry.

I was young enough, and unworldly enough, to believe that a young man crying was something so profoundly aberrant that it was beyond embarrassing—it was almost horrifying. And Randy's tears were, I suspected, not merely an inarticulate expression of his rage at his inability to handle what to most everyone else was a simple school assignment, but perhaps a more deep-seated lament at the self-imposed smallness of his own world. Lennie's dream of owning a farm and "living off the fatta the land" was modest enough in itself (hence the significance of his last name)—but even this dream proved futile as he dies at the hands of his best friend, George Milton, in what can only be characterized as a mercy killing. Perhaps Randy was thinking that his destined life as a coal miner was itself a kind of death sentence—as, very likely, it was.

And so he cried. Not loudly or histrionically, but with an appalling silence that showed only in his crumpled face and the thick drops that fell from his eyes.

What else could I do but take him in my arms?

Once again, I felt myself falling into the stereotyped female role of comforter of the male species. That was what women did—what they were for—wasn't it? I won't say that at the time I was all that feminine. I didn't take much care of my dirty blond hair, which I merely tied back in a long ponytail to keep it out of my face. But I like to think that I had (and still have) a nice-looking oval face with soft, gentle features and a lean body with only a modest endowment at the chest but with long, athletic legs made strong by repeated exercise (I was really good on the uneven bars). I almost never wore a skirt or a dress, but this time I happened to be wearing a simple print dress that my mother had made—only because the late September weather was still warm enough that I wanted something cool and airy on my person.

Randy had been sitting in a kind of lotus position, so I had no choice but to squat down on his lap and take his head in my arms. The result was that his head became nestled between my small breasts while I had to spread my legs around either side of him. Somehow the sexual suggestiveness of the position escaped me in my almost frantic quest to dry those dreadful man-tears.

I could feel those tears wetting my chest as Randy's arms wrapped themselves almost convulsively around my waist. Somehow the contact with my body acted like an emotional trigger for him, and he uttered a wail that would surely have been heard through the door of my bedroom and reached my mother's ears if his face hadn't been muffled by my breasts. Now really alarmed, I could do nothing but coo, "It's okay, it's okay," over and over again, as if those silly, meaningless words might have some sort of incantatory effect.

To this day I don't know how the rest happened. I casually noted the growing erection in his groin, but paid it little attention: I figured it was a natural and unconscious by-product of the male anatomy, and becoming intimate with him was the furthest thing from my mind. But apparently it wasn't from Randy's.

In some mysterious fashion he managed to pull his member out of his sweat pants and, pushing my thin cotton panties aside at my own groin, insert himself into me.

At first I didn't even understand exactly what was happening. Oh, I was of course familiar with the basics of copulation— even in the complete absence of anything that could be called sex ed in my conservative high school—but only as something that was done with suitable privacy and under the cover of darkness, not at 3:30 in the afternoon and with my mother bustling cluelessly in the kitchen not more than twenty feet away beyond a closed but unlocked door.

It was only when Randy broke through the impediment he encountered as his organ probed me that I suddenly realized what was going on. Strangely enough, aside from the rupture of that ridiculous little membrane I felt little pain, even though I'd listened with awe and wonder as some of my friends described the exquisite agony of being "entered" for the first time—the first several times—by their importunate boyfriends. And another anomaly of the unconventional position we had unwittingly adopted was that I was in charge of the proceedings—or could have been if I had been more aware of the scenario. Instead, Randy had to do most of the work while awkwardly seated on the floor, at times seizing my hips and moving me up and down as if I were an immense yo-yo.

It was all over in a few minutes. The grunts that came from him, and the sudden surge of wetness that filled me, testified to the less than climactic completion of the act, at least as far as I was concerned. In fact, I can't think of anything less erotic than what had just happened, given that we had remained all but fully clothed during the whole episode and Randy hadn't taken the slightest interest in my feelings, physical or emotional.

And yet, he continued to cling to me—and to rest his head on my breasts—after it was over. I had to pry myself away from him, and he wasn't keen on letting me go. When I did so, getting up stiffly and sitting heavily on the bed nearby, he seemed irrationally embarrassed at the exposure of his softening member and quickly shoved it back into his pants. I just sat there looking down at him, not knowing what I was feeling.

We said nothing. After what seemed an interminable interval, I realized that I needed to clean myself up lest I stain my dress and the bedsheets I was sitting on. With only a touch of awkwardness, I peeled off my stained panties and threw them away into a far corner of the room, then dabbed my crotch with some Kleenex. There wasn't much blood there, but there was some.

"We shouldn't have done that," I said slowly.

"Why?" he said, looking dreadfully vulnerable, his face still streaked with tears.

"We just shouldn't have," I said. I didn't want to tell him that there was mercifully little chance of my getting pregnant: I knew my cycle well enough to know that it would be at least a week or more before I began ovulating. But I didn't want to convey the impression that he could just "have" me at the snap of his fingers and without any consequences.

"You . . . hadn't done it before," he said—and he couldn't keep a soupçon of pride from entering his voice.

"Of course not," I said impatiently, although I was well aware that a fair number of girls in high school made no bones about being "experienced."

"I hadn't either," he said softly, and somehow that surprised me. True, I hadn't seen him with any other girl, but somehow I just assumed that boys "did" it as soon as they possibly could, with whoever was willing.

When I said nothing to his confession, he uttered the words that changed our relationship forever.

"I love you."

Even at sixteen, I knew that he really didn't mean those words—he may have thought he did, but he didn't. It was the sex talking. Contrary to popular myth, boys of that age are perhaps even more inclined to romanticize sex than girls are. But as he gazed up at me with that somber, vulnerable look that I would come to know so well over the years, I knew I had to be careful what I said in reply. My first instinct had been to scoff derisively ("Oh, come off it, Randy, don't be ridiculous!"), but I was well aware that that would crush him emotionally and perhaps make him permanently unable to express himself un-affectedly to another human being.

So I slid off the bed, sat down next to him, stroked his face with my hand, and said, "Randy, that's really sweet. I don't know what I feel about you yet, but let's see how it goes."

I'd spoken the truth. I *didn't* know what I felt about him—I simply didn't know him well enough. Our families were casual-ly acquainted—our respective fathers more than our mothers—but that was about all.

My noncommittal remark was enough for Randy, and he beamed at me. I almost thought he was going to start crying again; and even though they might have been happy tears, I'm not sure I could have dealt with them.

Instead, he hugged me in a curiously chaste manner, seem-ing to make an exaggerated effort not to have his chest touch my breasts. And yet, there was a look in his eyes that suggested he might want more action right away—but I put a stop to that.

I got up hastily and said, "I think you'd better go home. Mom's getting dinner ready." That was an outright lie: even Mom didn't start preparing our evening meal at four in the af-ternoon. But Randy took it in good stride. Getting up swiftly, he grabbed his books, stuffed them in a frayed backpack, and prepared to leave the room and the house.

But he turned around at the door to my bedroom. I was right behind him, expecting him to walk through. Instead, he looked down at me (he was about three inches taller than me), bent his head down, and gave me a feathery kiss on the mouth. His lips fluttered as they touched mine, and I think a shiver racked his entire frame—and mine too—as he kept his lips lightly fastened to my own for what seemed like an eternity, but could surely have been no more than a few seconds.

Then he went home.

That's how it started. Our unexpected encounter had, for better or worse, created a bond that would last forever, and I'd never be able to think of him the same way as I'd done before. It was quite obvious that he wanted to take things to another level, at least physically. And why not? No doubt he'd enjoyed himself that first time—but he probably had a reasonable expectation that he would enjoy himself a lot more with suitable preparation.

And preparation of a different sort was on my agenda also. I'm referring to birth control. I wasn't so naïve as to think that Randy (I tried not to think what a horrible pun his very name had become) would be content with the "rhythm method," forswearing sex for a week or two every month; and I also doubted that he would have the discipline to wear a condom every time.

So I had a frank and open talk with my mother, who responded with a kind of blasé resignation, as if knowing that such a conversation was bound to happen sooner or later. We country folk start procreating early, and it was not unusual for both boys and girls in our tiny high school to drop out to get married or even to continue in school with a baby in tow. Mom urged me to get an IUD and even accompanied me to the one medical clinic in town.

It was evident that Randy was keen on resuming our physical union, and he made it clear that his own house was pretty much off-limits for such activity: his parents were very religious and were among the few who openly objected to premarital sex, so we'd have to meet at my house exclusively. My own mother, as I've suggested, didn't seem to care one way or the other, and my father was too exhausted from his back-breaking work at the mine to pay much attention to the fact that his only daughter now seemed to have a beau.

I remember the first time I stripped naked in front of Randy. He had taken off his own clothes in a kind of manic alacrity, and I had to admit that what I saw pleased and impressed me. Lean as he was, he was muscular in all the right places, and there was an imposing strength in his broad shoulders and pillar-like legs. I also sensed—not that I had the least experience in the matter—that his member was a bit larger than average. As I tried to keep up with his nudity with a hesitant and not entirely comfortable striptease of my own, I saw him devour me with his eyes almost like a predatory animal focusing on a kill. Maybe that's unkind, but given that no other male—not even my father—had seen me naked for a decade, I think my unease was not unwarranted.

But he proved to be a tender and considerate lover, even though he had to be laboriously instructed the mysteries of female desire. Indeed, I half sensed that he wasn't even fully aware that women had orgasms just as much as men did; and when I had my first climax in his presence, he seemed to gaze upon me with a kind of appalled fascination, as if he was witnessing something inexpressibly obscene.

Let me be frank, however: I think I was the more willing to couple with Randy because I knew in my heart that, no matter what I felt for him or he for me, our relationship was destined to be temporary.

I've already mentioned that my parents had long ago determined that I should eventually seek my way out of Dunsmuir, both for my sake and theirs. There was a whole big world out there, and they were intent on my partaking of at least a little of it. They knew that they had missed the chance of doing so, and they were keen on ensuring that I had a radically different kind of life. My very gender made me unsuitable for work at the mine, and the town offered little else for a bright, ambitious young woman.

But everyone—I, my parents, Randy's parents, and Randy himself—knew that, whether he finished high school or not, his sole destiny was the mine.

He accepted his fate unquestioningly and without resentment. Dunsmuir was the only world he knew, and he didn't seem much interested in anything else. Maybe it's unkind of me to attribute such a narrowing of horizons to him, but he really didn't exhibit the least interest in what was going on in other communities, other states, or other parts of the country, let alone the world as a whole. In this he wasn't at all unusual in our town—and probably in most towns in this nation and elsewhere. Cosmopolitanism is not easily acquired.

And I admit the sex was good. After I had patiently taught Randy how to please me as well as himself, we had a very nice time. Like the average oversexed teenage boy, Randy was capable of performing over and over again, and sometimes I had trouble keeping up with him. I'll also mention—and no more than mention—that he developed a penchant for what is tactfully called "rear entry." I can't say I was thrilled at this uncomfortable and occasionally painful procedure, but I went along with it—only on condition that Randy repay me by doing things that I liked.

It became quickly obvious to everyone at school that we were a couple engaged in regular sex. And we were by no means the only ones. Among the fifty or so people in our junior class, at least half were similarly involved. The girls with sexual experience formed an informal club or clique, speaking among themselves with purportedly world-weary fatigue about the tedium of pleasing their insatiable mates—although in reality, they would have been the first to whine if those mates deserted them or wanted to be "just friends." And there were any number of breakups, philandering by both boys and girls, and many of the other relationship troubles that adults are constantly dealing with. Meanwhile, the boys and girls who still remained virgins looked upon us with a confusing mix of awe, envy, jealousy, resentment, and fear.

Initially the "club" had trouble accepting me as one of their number: after all, I had long ago developed the reputation as a tomboy (not to mention a science geek), so a number of the girls—who were doing everything they could, with makeup, revealing clothes, and what they took to be seductive poses, to let their classmates know they were "getting it"—were incredulous that I had managed to snag a boy of my own. And even though neither Randy nor I engaged in the vulgarity of talking about our intimacies, it became so obvious that we were physically involved that I found myself in the "club" whether I wanted to be or not.

I don't wish to convey the impression that having sex was all that Randy and I did; but I will say that, in our little town, there wasn't much else to do. We had exactly two movie theatres—strangely enough, they were across the street from each other on Main Street, our only major commercial thoroughfare—but they didn't even have first-run movies, instead doing a surprisingly brisk business showing older films (sometimes vintage black-and-white films from the 1940s or earlier) that attracted both adults and kids. Dunsmuir was also not noted for parks, malls, or even playgrounds where young people could congregate. Sometimes Randy and I drove to Fenton, which had a few more facilities to interest us; he was already an expert and efficient driver, and both his parents and mine had no compunction letting him sit behind the wheel of their respective cars.

But as junior year ended, summer vacation was over, and senior year began, our breakup became imminent. Nothing was said, but I'm sure both of us knew what was coming. I was going to college, he was going to the mine—and that would be the end of it.

I had a feeling that he actually wanted to propose to me, but knew that my response would be no—and that might mean the end of our sexual sessions, something he couldn't contemplate without acute agony. And so he became even more sullen and taciturn than usual as the fall turned to winter. Sometimes I felt that he was becoming a bit rougher in bed as a way of punishing me for my impending desertion—of him, of the town, and of the only life he knew or wanted to know.

Of course, my college choices were limited. For financial reasons, an in-state institution was the only option. My family had once taken a trip to the Finger Lakes—one of the few times we took a vacation anywhere—and I was thrilled at what seemed a whole new world of truly civilized life that opened up before me; but I had little hope of getting into Cornell, although I did make an application to Wells College in Aurora (I didn't get in). In the end, Lehigh and Penn State accepted me, as did a few other, smaller colleges; and paradoxically I chose Lehigh as being closer to home. I was ready to leave—but not ready to go to the ends of the earth.

After a humdrum graduation from high school, Randy and I continued our liaisons during a languid summer. He tried desperately not to think of our impending separation—and, in all honesty, I didn't either. The physical and psychological benefits of regular sex are not to be underestimated. But almost immediately after graduation Randy had taken up his humble place in the mine, and in our meetings he already seemed covered with coal dust—and, more plangently, with the sense of hopelessness that came with a harsh, grinding, dead-end job. He now clung to me with an unspoken desperation, as if I were his one fragment of sanity and pleasure as he faced a lifetime of relentless toil.

I remember how he looked glumly on that late August day when I packed my few belongings and loaded them into the family car (I didn't have my Mini then), my mother impatiently waiting for me to finish so that she could whisk me away from the town that had become as much of a soul-crushing prison to her as it was to her husband. It was as if Randy couldn't believe I was actually going through with it: the whole business of leaving for college seemed to him some cruel ruse or practical joke I was playing on him as payback for some imaginary blunder on his part.

I wished that my mother wasn't looking on sharply as I gave Randy a final hug, but she seemed inclined to think I might irrationally change my mind and bolt from the scene—although why I would so heedlessly throw away my ticket out of this place I couldn't for the life of me imagine. Randy, as if exacting some minimal revenge on my mother for not letting us say goodbye in private, gave my bottom a deliberate squeeze as I muttered insincerely, "Take care of yourself."

He said nothing—for what, indeed, could he say that wouldn't sound fatuous or resentful or bitter?

And so we parted.

Nevertheless, I wasn't quite so unkind as to turn my back on him altogether. When a girl lets a guy enter her body repeatedly over a period of two years, an emotional bond of some sort has to be created. Did I love him? Maybe—as much as a sixteen- or seventeen-year-old girl can be said to know what love really means. And maybe I wanted to let Randy down easy. He knew I wasn't prepared to go from being a coal miner's daughter to a coal miner's wife; but I did wish to convey that he had meant something to me—as in fact he had.

So I wrote occasional letters to him, and even spoke to him on the phone a few times. Randy wasn't exactly very good at correspondence, and I found his short, misspelled letters—written on lined paper with big block letters—both amusing and inexpressibly sad. That first year of college so expanded my whole outlook on life that, when I came home that summer (for where else did I have to go?), I already felt a different person.

But I made the mistake of resuming relations with Randy. It was a mistake because he himself tried to preserve the illusion that nothing had changed—that I'd just gone inexplicably away on a long vacation and was now back, and we could just pick up where we left off. I will be frank and say that I did miss our regular sex—I was entirely celibate during that first year at Lehigh—and the feel of his naked body next to mine was something of a tonic for me, as it clearly was for him. I hope I don't sound uncharitable in saying that he didn't seem even infinitesimally different from when I had left him nine months before—except, perhaps, that he already seemed worn down by his thankless work just as my father had been in his twenty-odd years underground.

That summer was such a nightmare—filled with the undeniable physical and emotional satisfaction of sex but, for me, a horrible sense that I was being dragged back to a life I was desperate to escape, even if it meant repudiating everyone and everything I had ever known—that I knew I couldn't repeat it. So when I returned to school, I was determined that I would never see Dunsmuir again except for the briefest of visits.

And I did it by the simple, if contemptibly passive-aggressive, tactic of not coming home during the summers. I somehow managed to get a succession of menial positions in Allentown and a succession of fleabag sublets that cost next to nothing and whose various deficiencies I could endure for a few months. I pretended to myself that I really needed to stay near the college to study more and get a head start on next year's classes—but it was really just to avoid Randy.

No, that's not fair. Randy had become a symbol of my hometown—a place whose tragically limited opportunities condemned its denizens to lives of quiet despair and early death. I not infrequently felt selfish in making sure I'd made a clean break from Dunsmuir. But I had my hands sufficiently full making my own declaration of independence: how would I be able to drag others with me, whether it be Randy or my parents or anyone else?

So the letters and phone calls stopped. I had casual involvements with various men at college, but they led nowhere. That didn't disturb me, for I wasn't looking forward to early marriage and the narrowing of horizons that can frequently bring with it. Meanwhile, I worked hard on my chemistry degree and had some hope of making a career of it. The death of my father put more than a damper on things, and my mother's failure to attend my graduation didn't help; but I walked away with that degree in hand and felt that there were abundant opportunities for me.

And yet, here I was, back in Dunsmuir. Maybe it would only be for the summer, as I hunted for a full-time job. But was it possible that this town had so deeply entered into the fabric of my being that it would never let me escape?

3

The door to Randy's house was opened by Andy.

I haven't mentioned her, have I?

Andrea was Randy's fraternal twin, and so inevitably everyone called her Andy. When they were growing up, they seemed inseparable—in some ways almost uncannily so. Everyone knows how close twins are—intellectually, emotionally, psychically—but Randy and Andy carried their similarities to unusual lengths. Let me be clear that Andy wasn't in any sense a tomboy: as a little girl she was radiant, wide-eyed, and doll-like, and she matured into a young woman whose beauty of face and figure would have attracted men of every stripe; but she seemed intent on restricting her interest and devotion to her twin brother.

And that's why it cut her to the quick when, as they both entered puberty, Randy began to show a transparent and at times cruel discomfort with and contempt for Andy, finding her constant presence a nuisance as he sought to emphasize his nascent manliness by hanging out with his male friends and eyeing the girls in school (including myself) with unabashed carnal desire. It was probably more than just this painful rejection by her twin that caused the emotional problems she subsequently suffered, but the upshot of it was that her schoolwork suffered so much that she was "held back" a grade, falling a full year behind Randy.

In high school, when I paid attention to her at all, I found her a strangely disturbing and unwelcome presence—a female echo of the man/boy who had chosen me for his sexual attentions. In spite of the emotional distance he attempted to establish between himself and her, they still seemed unnaturally close—rather like two facets of a single personality. Incredible as it may seem, she and I hardly spoke more than a few sentences to each other in all the two years that Randy and I were involved. Part of that had to do with the fact that he and I spent most of our time at my house, when we weren't out on the town. His own parents—stern, humorless, God-fearing folk—made their disapproval of our involvement abundantly plain; but so long as our shenanigans weren't occurring under their roof, they didn't seem overly concerned.

So it didn't entirely surprise me to see that Andy had, by default, now insinuated herself back into Randy's life. No doubt she had finished high school in as undistinguished a manner as she had entered it, and now that the major obstacle between her twin and herself—me—was out of the picture, she could re-ingratiate herself into Randy's affections. I don't mean to suggest there was anything calculated in all this; she was too naive for that. It was just that she couldn't imagine any kind of life that didn't involve her brother at the center of it.

When she saw me standing at her doorstep, her eyes widened momentarily in surprise and alarm, then returned to their habitual cowlike placidity. She may have been taken aback at seeing me, but I suspect she felt (correctly) that I was in no way a threat to take Randy away from her again. Seeing her at the door, I thought she seemed more like Randy's young wife than his twin sister.

"Alison!" she said. "It's good to see you." After a pause she added ingeniously and without malice, "I didn't think you'd ever come back here."

"I didn't think I would either," I said frankly. "But this is the first chance I've had to see my mom after . . . what happened to my dad."

She bowed her head mechanically in respect and said, "I'm sorry about that." It was as if she felt some personal responsibility for my father's passing.

"Thank you," I said. "Is Randy here?"

"Yes. Yes, of course he is."

And she opened the door more widely and let me in.

Their house was small and, to put a kindly spin on it, cozy: a living room with obviously used and somewhat woebegone furniture, a dining room that scarcely had room for a square table that could seat no more than four people, and a kitchen that seemed right out of the 1950s. It seemed to have only one bedroom, and a shudder went through me at the thought that brother and sister had gone back to sharing a bed as they had done when they were children. I very much doubted that any sexual irregularities were going on: maybe Randy magnanimously slept on the couch in the living room, although it didn't seem big enough to accommodate his lanky frame comfortably.

Randy himself was, to my surprise, in the kitchen washing up after dinner—something I never recalled him doing in high school. Of course, his mother did that work, but somehow I figured he'd have insisted on his sister taking over that role in this peculiar household. In any case, he had no doubt heard the door open and chatter of female voices, so he quickly washed his hands on a dishrag and came out to see who had so unexpectedly invaded his home and hearth.

When he saw me he stopped in his tracks for a second, his face blank; then he shuffled slowly in my direction. I saw that he had to swallow hard before he could speak a word to me.

All he said was, "Ali?"

In that single word—that nickname that no one else used—I could sense the confusing mix of hurt, disappointment, anger, desire, and futile expectation that summed up our relationship, or at least his understanding of our relationship. In that moment it became crystal clear to me that he had not sought out any other woman for his favors after I had abandoned him, and my sudden and unexpected return seemed to kindle in him a faint flicker of hope that I had, after four long years, seen the error of my ways and now yearned to return to his embrace. I think he knew even then—and knew even after what subsequently happened—that this was a pipe dream, but there wasn't much else in his life to lift him out of the treadmill of drudgery into which he had already fallen.

"Hi, Randy," I said neutrally. "It's good to see you."

We approached each other like a divorced couple who had unexpectedly run into each other at some public event and had to maintain at least the semblance of civility. He rubbed suddenly sweaty palms against his rough jeans and took me gently in his arms, holding me as if I were a piece of porcelain that would break upon the slightest pressure. When I did not in fact break, he held me a little tighter, enjoying the press of my breasts against his chest. For my part, I wasn't about to throw my arms around his neck in typical lost-girlfriend fashion, but held him awkwardly around his waist until he finally let me go.

Randy was, of course, inhibited in his display of affection by the presence of Andy, who peered at us with an unflinching gaze and an unreadable expression.

"You're looking good," I said. "Both of you," I added, casting a glance at Andy.

The remark was largely formulaic. In fact, Randy wasn't looking so good—he already had the eternally dusky, beaten-down look that miners of twenty years' standing seem to get, and the fact (I assumed it to be a fact) that he wasn't enjoying even the primitive if redeeming pleasure of regular sex made him appear more sullen and glum than usual. Andy, on the other hand, had blossomed into a really beautiful creature— her fresh, open countenance, trim but shapely figure, and a rudimentary skill at applying makeup made her seem like one of those perfect housewives out of a 1950s commercial, doing housework in high heels while keeping every strand of hair in place. That hair of hers—jet black, lavishly styled in something close to an archaic beehive, and accentuating her oval face with its flawless and gentle features—was striking, but no more so than the rest of her. It would be cruel of me to say that she had attained her heart's desire: to keep her beloved twin brother attached to her apron-strings in as close to a pseudo-marriage as two siblings could manage.

Randy wasn't impressed by my remark. Hardly casting his eyes in my direction, he said, "You're looking good too."

They led me to the sofa, where I sat down. Randy pointedly did not sit next to me, but lowered himself heavily into a frayed easy chair near the fireplace. It was Andy who sat demurely at the other end of the sofa, as if forcing her brother to compare the relative charms of the two women in his life.

"How's work going?" I said, just to have something to say.

Once again Randy didn't take the bait. "It's going," he said, scarcely opening his mouth.

Andy jumped in. "Randy's really working hard at the mine!" she chirped in her flutelike voice. "He comes home so tired, he hardly has the energy for anything." The implication was clear: *Certainly no energy to go out on the town and bed down with unwelcome females.*

Randy didn't seem to appreciate Andy's comment and tried to steer the conversation in a different direction. "Why've you come back?" he said bluntly, with no little tinge of hostility and resentment.

"Well," I said, trying to keep my tone even, "this is the first chance I've had to come here since my father died. I just wanted to see how Mom was doing. I don't expect to stay long."

Randy digested this with a kind of weary resignation. I could tell that Andy was also hanging on to my every word.

"That was too bad," he said dully.

"Yeah, it must have been," I said. "Maybe you can tell me about it."

The request seemed to take him aback, and he looked up at me sharply, gazing into my eyes for the first time. "I don't know anything about it," he said evasively.

"You don't?" I said, surprised. "Surely you were at the mine when it happened. My mom—"

"*I wasn't!*" he shouted at me.

There was a cavernous silence.

"You weren't there?" I said uncomprehendingly. "How is that possible? Were you sick that day?"

Randy suddenly leapt to his feet and started pacing the room, making sure to keep as far away from me as possible. He made a fist with his right hand and started punching it into the palm of his left.

I was beginning to wonder if he would ever say another word, so I said, "Randy, can you—"

"It was at night," he interrupted.

"At *night?*" I said, astounded. "Nobody works at the mine at night. Maybe they did once, but certainly not when my dad was there. How—?"

"I don't think he died at the mine," Randy almost whispered.

This was going from bad to worse, and I was starting to get

dizzy and confused. There was a sick feeling at the pit of my stomach.

Randy was still walking around furiously, looking for all the world as if he were trying to find some reason—any reason—to bolt from the premises. I got up stiffly and went over to him, making him stop his relentless pacing by putting my hands on his shoulders. Then I forced him to look me in the face and said:

"Randy, please tell me what you know. I can't get anything out of Mom—she claims not to have the slightest idea about what happened. I need to know, Randy. Please tell me."

With each word I had gotten more choked up, until toward the end I could hardly speak. My eyes were filled with tears, and I desperately blinked them away.

Randy could only gaze at me with a bizarre mix of terror and frustration in his face. He himself looked as if he were on the verge of bursting into tears—just as he had done years ago in my bedroom when he had taken my virginity. He bit his lip so hard that I thought he might draw blood; then finally he said almost inaudibly:

"I don't know what happened. There was something strange . . . We only heard about it the next morning. Even then none of the foremen told us—it got around by word of mouth. I can't remember what anyone said. I think someone mentioned"—and here he paused, looking away from me as if fearful of my reaction—"he was burned."

"Burned?" I said incredulously. "How's that possible? Was there a fire in the mine?"

"I don't know, I tell you!" he almost shrieked, coming close to breaking out of my grasp. "It's just what someone said."

"You didn't see the body?"

"No, of course not. It was taken right to the funeral home."

Knowles Funeral Chapel was the only such establishment in the city. Given the town's aging population, I imagine it did a brisk business.

I shook my head in disbelief. "I don't get it. Surely there must have been some kind of announcement by the overseer—"

"There wasn't," Randy interrupted truculently.

"—or some investigation by the Bureau of Mines? I mean," I said with ever-growing exasperation, "a person can't just *die* in a mine and nothing happen!"

We were now staring at each other, breathing stertorously as if we were two boxers taking a break from a particularly arduous confrontation. Andy was gazing up at us with a stunned expression, wondering who would prevail in this bizarre conflict of words.

"I don't know," Randy said, looking away from me in a kind of defeat, as if taking the blame for the whole perplexing situation.

I continued to glare at him, hoping I was not creating the impression that I was holding him personally responsible for what had happened to my dad—and, more, the inexplicable aftermath.

"I think we need to look into this," I said tartly. That "we" was, as I well knew, more than a little bit of wishful thinking. My mother had made it clear that her ignorance of the matter was willful and inveterate, and Randy really didn't have the time, interest, or resources to help me. Maybe he wanted to—chiefly as a way of rekindling his interest in me, or rather of hoping that my interest in *him* might be rekindled—but neither he nor I could see what he could actually do.

I already had some ideas, and I vowed to put them into action the next day.

I didn't stay much longer at Randy and Andy's house. I will frankly say their place gave me the creeps: their living situation was not healthy, and Randy seemed not to have the slightest perception that his twin sister had cocooned him within her own orbit in a way that might make it impossible for him to break away and form anything approaching a healthy relationship with another woman. So far, Andy didn't regard me as a threat, taking at face value my affirmation that I wouldn't remain in town very long. But if she detected any wavering from that resolution on my part, I had little doubt that she would turn her venom on me with all the ruthlessness of a mama bear protecting her cubs.

4

The next day I was at the doorstep of the public library only minutes after it opened.

The small, one-story brick building housed a surprising number of books. The "historical" part of the edifice—it dated to around 1880—was still in use, but a surprising influx of funds about fifty years ago, at a time when the Pennsylvania state budget was fleetingly in a surplus, had resulted in a ungainly, utilitarian, but serviceable addition that allowed the library to expand both its stock of books and its general services. Those services now of course included any number of computer terminals for Internet access, plenty of audio books and ebooks, and other novelties that seemed destined to replace the printed word. But successive generations of doughty librarians in this backward-looking town, correctly feeling that these newfangled fripperies were not likely to appeal to the tiny slice of the population that actually read books, maintained the print collection with the air of making a final, perhaps futile, stand for civilization against the tide of digital barbarism.

But it wasn't exactly the books, or even the magazines, that I was interested in. Nodding to the head librarian, Betsy Farmer (she had only one salaried assistant, aside from an ever-shifting parade of elderly female volunteers), who had held the fort for at least two decades, I headed to the basement, where bound files of the town's one newspaper were dutifully housed.

The *Dunsmuir Republican* was, as its name suggests, founded shortly after the Civil War, and by some miracle it had continued publication to the present day. It aggressively preserved its partisan name long after the majority of the townsfolk had shifted its own political allegiance, but several decades ago it did bow to economic reality to the extent of lapsing into once-a-week publication. That was fine with me; in fact, I assumed it would make my job a bit easier.

What I wanted to do, at least at the start, was to look up any article about my father's death and burial.

I found it hard to imagine that there wouldn't be *something* written on the subject: what else did the paper have to write about? When I was living here, I paid scant attention to the weekly paper as it landed lightly (it usually contained only eight pages, sometimes expanding to a luxurious twelve if ad revenue picked up fleetingly) on our doorstep every Tuesday evening. Now and again I would flip through it to see what movies were playing in town, but that was about it. I passively noticed various reports on mine activities—and accidents—but they were usually worded so blandly that they made little impression on me. After all, why should I care—as a child, or even a teenager—about what happened at the mine, so long as my daddy was safe?

But now my daddy was dead. And I wanted to know why— or at least how.

The paper had begun as an enormous bedsheet, almost three feet long and one and a half wide; but over the past several decades it had shrunk to the size of the freebie papers you see in so many small towns, published mostly for the advertisements or to announce the usual array of flower shows, church meetings, and school closings that would interest a community that paid little attention to the baffling events of the wider world. But the library continued to bind even these un-newsworthy issues in stiff brown boards, as if posterity would really find a need to consult them in the years and decades to come.

The issues for 2016 had been bound only recently, and in spite of its recency it was evident that no one had consulted this volume. As I pried open the front cover, it crackled a bit, as if protesting the disturbance of its coma-like repose. I had to believe the death of my father had been noted in at least a brief article—and, sure enough, that is what I found in the April 3 issue:

> MARCH 31.—Guy Mannering, 45, a veteran of more than twenty years at the Brashear mine, was found dead yesterday evening at the western entrance to the mine. Cause of death was not immediately evident, according to the medical examiner, William Baxter. The body was taken to the Knowles Funeral Chapel in preparation for interment.

That was it. This almost insultingly laconic piece raised more questions than it answered. First, it alerted me to the existence of a "western entrance" to the mine that I had never heard of before, since I had assumed the only entrance was the one to the east, where I knew my father had trudged every day of his working life. Second, it confirmed Randy's perplexing comment that Daddy had died *at night,* but it gave no reason for why he would have been there hours after the workday was over. The third puzzling thing was the absence of any stated cause of death. Okay, the reporter (whoever it was—the article was unsigned) may have failed on that morning of March 31 to get any definitive word from the apparently tight-lipped Mr. Baxter; but the paper had not gone to press for several days, so why wasn't there any follow-up report providing more—or any—information?

I checked the papers for the next several weeks—indeed, several months—and there was nothing more about why Daddy had died. Nothing.

Something was very wrong here.

What could my father have been doing at the mine in the evening? The mine's output had dwindled inexorably over the decades as one vein of coal after the other had been exhausted, and there was no reason why anyone would want or need to work at the mine beyond the normal 8–5 workday. Had he gone alone—or were there others with him? Had there been some kind of fight or argument? Daddy wasn't exactly a drink-ing man, so I found it hard to imagine him getting involved in a drunken brawl.

Other questions plagued me, uppermost being this: *Why hadn't Mom been more insistent on being told something— anything—about how Daddy had died?* She seemed deliberately and perversely obtuse on the subject, as if she didn't want to get to the bottom of the matter. Didn't she *care* what had hap-pened to her husband of twenty-two years? The moment that thought flitted into my brain, I suppressed it as unworthy of myself—and of her. Mom had never shown any sign of being other than a loving and devoted wife to my father, and I had no right to cast aspersions on her character. He was dead, after all; so perhaps her lack of curiosity was just a mental shield to pro-tect her from dwelling too painfully on unpleasant details. Knowing how or why Daddy died wouldn't bring him back.

But *I* had to know.

That medical examiner, William Baxter, didn't work in Dunsmuir; our town was too small and insignificant for that, as the receptionist at the police department—where I headed af-ter slamming shut that bound volume of the *Dunsmuir Repub-lican* and storming out of the library—informed me curtly. I would have to go to Fenton.

And that's where I went. I had no appointment, but Baxter's secretary apparently took pity on me—or perhaps she was alarmed at what might have been a glint of anger in my eyes—and, after putting me off for a minute, ushered me into Baxter's office and quickly retreated to her own workspace.

Baxter was a stout, balding man in his fifties, with a flabby, doughy face that seemed to quiver uncontrollably of its own accord. He looked up blandly—and perhaps, I thought, a little warily—at me and asked my business.

I got right to the point. "I'd like to see my father's death certificate. He died in the Brashear mine about a year and a half ago."

The doughy face suddenly firmed up with all the self-importance of the petty bureaucrat. "That won't be possible."

I was stunned. "But—but," I blundered, "isn't that a matter of public record? He's my *father!* Don't you think I have a right to know what happened to him?"

Baxter looked at me with an almost pitying gaze, as if speaking to a somewhat dim-witted ten-year-old. "I'm sorry for your loss, but the document you seek can only be obtained by court order, or in the course of legal proceedings."

"*What?*" I cried incredulously.

That patronizing look, with its wisp of a knowing smile, had become fixed on his face. "In the event that you wish to take legal action against the Brashear mine in a wrongful death suit, your lawyer would be permitted to make an application to secure the document. But"—and the wretch actually chuckled as he said this—"it is my understanding that Mr. Conrad Brashear has made quite a generous settlement with your family, so I am not sure that any further litigation would produce the desired results."

I stared at him with undisguised hatred. If looks could kill, this sorry specimen of humanity would be lying in a pool of his own fat on the floor of his tidy office.

But he knew he had the upper hand. So all I could do was to flounce out of his office with as much silent outrage and indignation as I could muster.

I was seething as I drove the few miles back to my house. But I wasn't going to be stopped. There were other ways I could find the information I was looking for. No, I wasn't going to break into Baxter's office in the dead of night and scour around his file cabinets or his computer for the document in question.

I was going to dig up my father's grave.

5

But I'd need someone's help for that. And who else could I turn to but Randy?

To say that I was conflicted about the whole matter would be putting it mildly. The least of my concerns was the frank illegality of violating my father's grave: that was a mere peccadillo, a necessary step in getting to the bottom of what was now coming to seem like a very bizarre event—or series of events. What concerned me far more was the fact that I would have to appear as a supplicant to my old boyfriend. How would he react to that? What exactly would I have to do to persuade him to engage in an act that might result in the loss of his own job and his very freedom? And would he interpret my appeal to him as a sign that my wayward affections had returned home exactly as I myself had done?

But I saw no alternative.

I waited till well after dinner—a dinner in which Mom, having cooked another huge and heavy meal, said almost nothing in the hope that she would not have to learn of what I had or had not found out about Daddy—to make my way over to Randy's house. For some reason I felt the need to wait till after dark, as if what I was about to propose was not fit for the light of day.

When I showed up at their place, I could see Randy and Andy through the thin curtain covering the glass-fronted door, sitting placidly on the couch stolidly watching television like an old married couple. It didn't seem to me that they were paying the slightest attention to the program—it was as if they had just turned on the TV and gazed at whatever happened to be on, too listless or uninterested even to change the channel on the remote.

Randy saw me even before I rang the doorbell and all but leaped up from the couch to let me in. I greeted him with a perfunctory hug, but he clung to me quite a bit longer than was necessary. He seemed to think that this second visit in as many days was a positive sign as far as he was concerned—and it wrung my heart to think that I might be using his own wish-fulfillment fantasies against him to serve my own ends.

I nodded nervously at Andy, who looked at me blankly from the couch. I didn't sense any actual hostility from her, just a nervous wariness: in antipodal contrast to her brother, she felt that my visit, while not immediately alarming, wasn't a good thing and bore close watching.

There was no way I could say what I had to say in her presence, so I disregarded her as best I could, looked Randy in the face, and said, "Can I speak to you privately, please?"

Randy's eyes expanded in a kind of delighted wonder, and a broad smile broke out on his face. At that moment he looked just like the teenager I had half fallen in love with in high school—the teenager who could really be a very sweet, kind, caring boy so long as he warded off his habitual sullenness and brooding melancholy. Without a word he ushered me with almost unseemly haste into the bedroom, Andy watching us fixedly all the way until Randy firmly closed and even locked the door behind us.

His eyes were shining, and he licked his lips in lascivious anticipation. He really couldn't be thinking I had come over for that purpose—but I suppose hope springs eternal in the male heart.

When I told him, frankly and baldly, what I wanted to do, he became white as a sheet.

Shaking his head furiously as if to dispel the vestiges of some hideous nightmare, he said harriedly, "No, no, we can't do that."

"We have to, Randy," I said, peering intently into his face. "It's the only way."

"But why?" he whined, suddenly sounding like a little boy befuddled by some incomprehensible command from his mother. "What good would it do?"

"I have to know. Something very strange is going on here, and I have to get to the bottom of it—at least as far as my father is concerned."

"You just have to let it go, Ali," he whispered.

"Why?" I spat back at him. "Why do I have to let it go? This is my *father*, Randy! What if it had been *your* father who had died? Would you have just 'let it go'?"

Maybe that was a little unfair. Randy's own father, also a coal miner, had taken disability after working for more than twenty years at the mine. Afflicted with emphysema from inhaling too much coal dust, he now sat at home with his patient wife, a taciturn casualty of this dismal industry.

"There must be some other way," Randy said, temporizing.

"I don't see how. Tell me another way, and I'll do it."

But he just shook his head, as if his mulish act of negation would free me of my unhealthy obsession over my father's remains.

It was then that I knew I would have to play my trump card. I'm not proud of what I did, but I couldn't think of any alternative at that moment.

I seduced him.

"Randy," I cooed, stroking his cool, bloodless face with my

hand, "you have to help me. Don't you remember all we've been through?—all the great times we had? Don't you remember?"

I kissed him full on the mouth. His own lips fluttered strangely against my own, and I could hear and feel him swallow painfully. For several moments it appeared as if Randy couldn't believe what was happening to him. He had wanted something like this for years, but the circumstances weren't exactly what he had imagined.

He seemed curiously reluctant to put his arms around my waist, but at last he did so, holding me lightly as if a firmer grip might cause him to be electrocuted. I slipped my hand from his face to his groin, where I could feel his member hardening even through the tough, unyielding fabric of his jeans.

I boldly stuck my tongue in his mouth, causing him to whimper from the unexpected sensation. After a time I broke off the kiss and, silently commanding him to be quiet (I wouldn't have been surprised if his sister was on the other side of the door where I had pinned Randy with my own body), I slid down to my knees.

The zipper of his jeans was quite stiff, and it took some effort to pull it down. After that, I tugged forcefully at both his jeans and his underwear, whipping both of them down to his knees. His organ bobbed in front of my face like a jack-in-the-box. I plunged it into my mouth.

Randy had to cover his mouth with his hand to prevent a gasp or cry from emerging from his throat. He knew as well as I that Andy would be aghast—startled, furious, despondent—if she knew what was going on in this cramped bedroom, but at the same time he was taken aback at the sudden realization of his years-long dream of renewing physical intimacy with me. Maybe he himself was aware that my actions weren't exactly disinterested, or an indication of my undying love for him; but at this moment he hardly cared.

I worked that thick member with all the skill I could muster, putting my lips, tongue, and even my teeth to the task of bringing him to quick satisfaction. And, indeed, it didn't take long, as the hot fluid gushed into my mouth.

Randy had long ago told me that he was particularly taken with this act because it was to his naively masculine mind a "sign of devotion," as he put it. Well, if that was all it took to elicit *his* devotion, I was happy to go along.

I stood up slowly and gazed at him. His eyes were still brightly shining as he seized my face with both hands and plastered a kiss on my mouth, as if he wished to taste the faint remnants of his own emission. But I had taught him well: he knew that it would be selfish if he were the only one to experience the ultimate pleasure, and so he slid a hand up my skirt (yes, I deliberately wore a skirt for the occasion), pulled away my panties from my crotch, and, holding me firmly upright with his other hand in the small of my back, stroked my wet sex in the way he knew from long experience would bring my own release.

And, by heaven, it did. I won't say I didn't enjoy it: I had gone through a fairly long sexual drought of my own, and the touch of a man's hand in that spot was not in any way unwelcome. As I now threw my arms, woman-fashion, around his neck and clung to him, he continued to minister to me until, in less time than it ordinarily took, he achieved his goal—and mine.

I attempted to muffle my own cries by burying my face in his neck—but there was something else that covered them up more effectively than I could have.

It was that curious sound—halfway between a groan and a moan, and originating in the general direction of the mine— that had been a regular feature of our lives ever since we could remember. But those words "groan" and "moan" weren't quite right—it was only by analogy that they could be used to describe what was really something unearthly, or at least non-human. It was no doubt our ingrained habit of anthropomorphizing everything we see, hear, and feel around us that made us think it was something human or even animate that was making those sounds.

Because they were so customary, if irregular—maybe once every two or three days, and always in the evening—we hardly paid attention to the noises: they just became a routine part of our existence, and we no more questioned them than we would have questioned the rotten-eggs smell of sulfur if we had lived in a place known for its hot springs. I remember that as kids some of my friends and I had once tried to identify even the location of the sounds, let alone their source; but we failed, and the matter didn't interest us enough—or seem consequential enough—for us to pursue the matter.

But the coincidence of the sounds with my orgasm almost caused me to burst out into giggling laughter. As it was, I managed to slap a hand over my mouth, my shining eyes fixed on Randy's in the sharing of this secret and obscene joke.

If you think that I was a manipulative bitch in so crassly using my body to get Randy to do what I wanted, you'd be right—but not entirely so. As I've mentioned before, I didn't love Randy; but during the two years of our intimacy in high school, I couldn't help feeling at least a reasonable facsimile of love, or at least tenderness, for him. And now, even after the passage of four years, I couldn't help sensing the ghost of the emotions—whatever, exactly, they might have been—I'd felt for him. I didn't envision a life with him; but he was sweet and kind, and his own stolid devotion to me touched me even if I couldn't reciprocate it.

So I got him to agree with my unholy plan. Not tonight—I needed to make some preparations first—but tomorrow. And of course Andy couldn't know.

We stepped out of his room like the guilty teenagers we felt, hoping to dodge a parent's disapproval after having made out in the privacy of a bedroom. Andy glared at us with an unreadable expression as we headed toward the front door: I suspect she knew what had happened, but I was also inclined to believe that she wouldn't confront Randy about it, hoping that I and my vixenish ways would simply disappear in due course of time and leave her once again free to dominate her twin brother's private life. I won't say that I didn't have the same hope.

*

The preparations didn't amount to much. I just needed to find two shovels—for of course I would assist Randy in our illegal exhumation, not caring to play the woman card and leave him to do all the work—and certain other implements that might be needed to open the actual casket. I won't deny that that phase of the undertaking caused a roiling in the pit of my stomach. For all my studies in chemistry—and in the related fields of biology and physiology—I was not accustomed to dealing with dead human bodies, and certainly not my own father. What would it look like after a year and a half of interment? It had presumably been embalmed: what effect would that have on the loathsome if necessary process of decomposition? None of this was worth thinking about, and I now wished that Randy and I had just plunged in and done the deed the night before: the thoughts that racked my brain through the course of the day were not pleasant.

I also knew that we would have to wait until well past midnight to make sure we could work undetected. The cemetery officially closed at sunset, but Randy informed me that some member of our tiny police force did make a casual inspection of the cemetery—or, more precisely, the quadrangle of streets that circumscribed it—in his patrol car at some unspecified point in the early evening. And God knows what hooligans or partygoers might be using the place for binge drinking or drug-taking in what was already promising to be a sweltering summer. In my high school years I'd never ventured into the boneyard for that or any other purpose, but I knew of other kids who did. With school out of session, the likelihood that rowdiness of some sort or other might occur there struck me as pretty high.

And how was Randy to evade detection by Andy in sneaking out of his house? He blithely assured me it wasn't a problem, and I had to take him at his word. I knew I would experience no difficulties, for my mother slept like the dead and her hoarse snores seemed to make the house shake. I doubted that even the noise of my starting my car would penetrate her thick cocoon of sleep.

And so I pulled up silently to Randy's house at around 1:30 A.M. that night, coasting to a near-stop on his gravel driveway and hoping that I wouldn't have to wait long for his emergence. I didn't: he was clearly on the lookout for me, and as soon as he saw my vehicle approach he slipped out the front door, closed it silently, and without a word slipped into the passenger seat.

We said nothing as we drove the short distance to Shady Haven. What was there to say? There was no small chance of our being arrested for what we were about to do—and Randy might well lose his job, meaning that he would be all but unemployable, since he had no other skill but mining. Was all this really worth the risk? It may have been for me, but now that I had roped Randy into it I felt a surge of guilt—a fear that

I would be ruining his whole way of life for a largely selfish purpose, and with little means to compensate him for the loss of his freedom and his livelihood.

Well, it just meant that we mustn't get caught.

The gate of the cemetery was closed, so we would have to park nearby and scale the low stone wall that surrounded it. I found an inconspicuous side street to leave my car, since it would obviously be disastrous if the vehicle were detected—by the police or anyone else—in close juxtaposition to the graveyard. The shovels and other tools made a disconcerting metallic clangor in our hands, as if already complaining about the immoral purpose to which they were about to be used.

I found the plot without difficulty. Looking down on it, with its bland headstone, I felt a complex mix of emotions—sadness, of course, at my father's early demise; puzzlement at the manner in which he had died; and, perhaps overriding them all, a sense of bitter frustration that he had come to the end of his life without much hope that his loved ones would remember him or pay due respect to the sacrifices he had made in his all too brief and circumscribed life. I remembered him, of course—but what about my mother, who had spent more than twenty years by his side, day and night? She had seemed unusually callous—even, inexplicably, frightened—about the cause of his death and seemed to resent my own refusal to let the matter rest. Was I being unfair to her? I hardly knew what to think, but I knew I couldn't stop my investigations now.

With a curt and silent nod, I indicated to Randy that we should start digging.

The task of unearthing a grave isn't nearly as easy as it might seem. Digging down six feet takes a substantial amount of energy, and I wasn't exactly used to manual labor. Randy, to my shame, threw himself almost mechanically into the task, heaving one shovelful of dirt after another into an irregular pile next to him while I did my best to preserve the layer of grass that we would have to put back in its place if we were to have any hope of even approximately concealing our act. The rhythmic cry of crickets resembled a weird sort of timepiece that was ticking off the moments as Randy descended inexorably into the hole he had created. I grudgingly had to acknowledge, looking at his sweat-covered face and the relentless movement of his muscular arms and shoulders, that there are some tasks a man is more suited for than a woman.

It must have taken nearly an hour of digging before Randy suddenly struck something other than dirt. I myself was now in the hole with him, resisting as best I could the vestigial sense that we were descending into the pit of hell. We glanced sharply at each other as Randy reached the surface of the coffin. The enormity of what we were doing seemed to overwhelm both of us at the same time, and I'm sure we both had to fight against a mad inclination to rush out of that hideous hole and fly from the scene, no matter how incriminating the telltale remnants of our handiwork might have been. So it was with a painful swallow and a renewed commitment to finish what we had started that I urged him to carry on.

We of course had to dig a hole wider than the coffin itself, if we had any hope of reaching the handles and prying the lid open. The smell of earth was itself foreboding, and I dispensed as mere hysterical delusion the intermingling of that aroma with some other, less definable stench. I mustn't let my emotions get the better of me, even if the act of exhuming the resting place of my own progenitor was about as obscene as anything could well be.

Randy completed the task and then hopped casually out of the pit. What would follow would be my task, and mine alone.

He glared blankly down at me as I silently pleaded with him for some kind of guidance or assistance. But he had lent all the assistance he intended to give; and if there were any revelations to come, appalling as they might be, they would be on my head.

The moment of truth had come—and I grimaced cynically to myself at the appropriateness of the expression. Regardless of the condition of the corpse, some kind of "truth" would no doubt be apparent—I suspected that it would not require a medical degree to give me at least some inkling of my father's fate. Why, then, was I so reluctant to undertake the final act and pull up the lid of the coffin? I again looked wide-eyed at Randy, an uncontrollable shiver running through my frame and actually making my teeth chatter. But he was no help, and now actually looked away from the scene of his labors: I would have to bear the full responsibility of what I was about to uncover.

When I did at last lift the lid, the sight that greeted me was not so much horrifying or loathsome as incomprehensible.

I did not see a rotting corpse, flesh melting away from the bones in spite of the embalming process. I did not see my father's face, blandly expressionless in death. I did not see my father's body wrapped in a suit that he would never have worn in life, shrinking around his frame as the inevitable course of decomposition did its silent work.

What I did see was a collocation of bones, scattered with insulting untidiness in a coffin far larger than necessary to house them. Some of the bones were fragmentary or mutilated—and a number of them clearly showed signs of *burning* at the tips. A more or less intact ribcage alone indicated that these remains were even human. They could have been the remains of anyone—nothing remained to indicate that they had been the osseous framework that had supported my father's flesh, organs, and mind in life.

And that was chiefly because there was no head at all—no skull, no jawbone, no nothing.

Interchapter 1: April 27, 1907

William Gainsford hadn't been able to sleep last night.

The meteor shower that seemed to pass directly over his house on the western edge of Dunsmuir had been unremitting, its countless bolts of penny-sized light and bewildering array of whizzing pellets awaking his newborn babe—a sturdy boy named Matthew whose already firm grip made him seem destined to follow his father's footsteps in wielding the pickaxe in the Brashear Mine—and alarming his weary and sleep-deprived wife, Jane. From time to time William had stepped to the bedroom window and watched the anomalous display, his gaunt, angular face lit up by the successive glimmers that seemed so near that he momentarily wondered if a fire might erupt in the dense forest that bordered his meager property.

But the day dawned like any other workday, and William put the night's turmoil behind him as he stoically ate the large breakfast his bleary-eyed wife dutifully prepared.

Before he made the mile-long trudge to the mine, however, he couldn't help making a brief detour into the forest. It wasn't every day the heavens bestowed such gifts, and he wondered if some remnant of the shower could be found. William's imagination did not often extend to the boundless cosmos, but on rare occasions he did give thought to what lay beyond the confines of this terraqueous globe. His father had been an amateur astronomer and even had a 3″ Bardou telescope into which William had peered every now and then; but he had been unable to grasp the titanic distances his father claimed separated the earth from even the nearest stars visible in the sky, and subsequent financial hardships had caused him to sell the instrument to a more prosperous neighbor.

It seemed he was in luck. Almost the moment he ventured into the forest he detected what he took to be something other than an earthly rock or pebble. How he could be so sure, he would not have been able to explain to himself; but the fact that it was slightly warm to the touch was a good indication. So warm was it, indeed, that William had to cradle it in a tuft of earth to protect his fingers from being singed.

He dumped the tiny visitor from the sky, earth and all, into his metal lunchbox and proceeded to work.

The rigors of the job made him all but forget his prize; but when the lunch whistle shrilled, he opened his lunchbox and, after initially being puzzled why there was a clod of earth there, remembered what he had done.

It was only when he had finished his lunch that he took the pellet in his hand. It was not entirely circular, seeming to have almost indistinguishable protrusions here and there; and now he was convinced that the grayish-white surface masked a glow deep within itself that reminded him of last night's shower. For a moment he wondered if money could be made from this minuscule object: maybe some scientist from a nearby college would find it worth at least a few dollars to possess it and subject it to whatever sort of analysis he might wish to undertake.

It was only after a few moments that William Gainsford began to scream.

As he held the thing in the palm of his hand, the flesh around the palm, and then around the fingers, began to melt away as if it had been doused with acid. Strangely enough, William did not experience any intense pain—or, indeed, any pain at all—but the horror of seeing his hand transformed in seconds into nothing but bone overwhelmed him.

He leaped up from his bench and, to the amazement and alarm of his colleagues, fled back into the mine. Wide-eyed and crazed—the destruction of his flesh had now proceeded up to his forearm—he careened against both men and equipment as he plunged sightlessly into the depths of his workplace. Slipping painfully against a piece of coal on the floor of the narrow corridor in which he found himself, he barged against a craggy wall of the mine and then, half-involuntarily, sent his body hurtling into a shaft whose impenetrable blackness and narrow confines caused his cry of terror and dismay to echo eerily before it was abruptly extinguished miles below.

William Gainsford was no longer aware that, in his mania, he had held onto that glowing pellet in what remained of his hand.

6

Somehow we managed to restore the gravesite to some semblance of how we had found it, although surely no one could have doubted—even after we clumsily put back the tufts of grass that we had set aside before we had begun digging in earnest—that the grave had been disturbed. The eerie silence pervading the place, aside from the omnipresent crickets, compelled us to finish our work with more haste than care, on the assumption that no one would be much concerned whether any ghoulish actions had occurred here or not.

The silence persisted as we drove back to Randy's house—but in this case, it was a silence caused by my own mental turmoil and by my partner's aggressive mask of ignorance. My hands shaking as they clutched the steering wheel, I flung harried and suspicious looks at Randy at random moments, but somehow couldn't face the thought of confronting him on what, if anything, he knew about this whole awful affair. Fragments of what Randy had grudgingly told me a few days ago—"I don't think he died at the mine" . . . "he was burned"—coursed through my mind, their import even more inexplicable than they had been when he had uttered them.

At last, pulling up quietly in front of his house, I blandly locked all the doors of the car just as he was about to exit without a backward glance or a single word. He tugged at the door handle as if repeated and increasingly agitated attempts to manipulate it would magically cause it to open. I let him wrestle with his embarrassment and discomfiture until he finally gave up and lay still, staring straight ahead of him into the dark.

"You knew what we were going to find, didn't you?" I said quietly.

"No, I didn't!" he whined, like a little boy being scolded by his mother.

"You knew the body had been burned."

"I *didn't* know! That's just what someone said. I couldn't make sense of it at the time myself. How could I? It was all just talk . . . no one really knew anything."

"Who told you that?"

"I can't remember . . . just one of the guys. I think"—and here he did glance slyly at me—"some of them weren't keen on telling me, because they knew we were friends and maybe it'd get back to your mom."

I passed over the euphemism ("we were friends") and said, "So you don't think Mom was told either?"

"How would I know?" he moaned. "I guess not. Haven't you talked to her about this?"

"Of course I have—but she seems to know less than you do."

Randy fell into a moody silence, looking at his hands. He seemed to be resentful that I was somehow blaming him for this whole series of events.

I got a sense that he really didn't know more than he was saying. Why should he? So I relented, unlocking the doors and patting him on the arm. "It's okay, Randy. It's not your fault. But," I added with grim determination, "I'm going to get to the bottom of this, and I hope you might help me somehow."

I wasn't even sure how he would do that. But that comment was enough for him to wheel around and paste a long, wet kiss on my mouth. It was as if he was reminding me that we had entered into physical intimacy again—whatever the reasons for that might have been—and that he therefore felt at liberty to renew the intimacy whenever he wished. Maybe I wasn't quite his "girl" again; but we'd touched each other's privates, and now I was enlisting him as an ally into whatever course of action I wanted to take. And that made us a couple, whether I liked it or not.

I pulled away from the kiss at last and said quietly, "Go home, Randy. And don't let Andy hear you."

He grinned at me boyishly as if we'd just come back from a make-out session. With a final, surprisingly gentle stroke of my cheek with his hand he almost leapt out of the car and made his careful way back into his house.

I did the same, and upon entering the front door I could still hear my mother snoring her head off. The time to confront her about all this would come, but not now.

*

And I wasn't sure it would come the next morning either.

Mom was up before I was—no surprise there, as I took the occasion to sleep in well past my usual time for rising. As I stumbled into the kitchen, she was placidly seated at the kitchen table drinking a cup of coffee, her own breakfast long finished.

She looked up at me blandly, then with faint alarm. "Gee, Alison, you don't look so good."

Thanks, Mom. "I didn't sleep very well."

She furrowed her brow, perhaps wondering whether I would take offense at her saying something maternal. "Coffee might help" was what she ended up saying.

"It sure would," I agreed heartily.

As I sat down with my own cup, earning another motherly frown because it was unaccompanied by any food, she said, "Anything troubling you?"

The comment seemed formulaic, but I couldn't help wondering if she had indeed heard my coming or going in the wee hours of the night. And I wondered even more what she really knew about my father's death—or, more pertinently, whether I could somehow pry that knowledge out of her.

I was too exhausted to try. She could be even more mulishly intransigent than Randy—and that's saying something. After a long and uncomfortable silence during which I managed to drain the cup of coffee but felt disinclined to take any more, or to engage in even idle chitchat with her, I got up from the table to take a long, hot, refreshing shower.

My course of action lay elsewhere. I needed more information—and it amused me to think that the person who might best help me was Andy.

I sauntered over to her house later that morning. Randy was safely at work and wouldn't return until dinnertime, and I doubted that housework or anything else took up so much of Andy's time that she couldn't spend a few hours doing my bidding.

I want to emphasize that I never disliked Andy—not in high school, and not now. How could I? She and Randy were so close that in some weird way I felt I had dated her just as I had dated her twin brother. Whatever umbrage she had taken at my monopolizing his time—and his body—back then had now dissipated, and she surely wasn't worrying that I would snatch him away from her clutches now.

When I knocked on her door, she opened it and gave me a broad smile. She seemed naively grateful that I had sought her out specifically, and that little jolt to her self-esteem lent an unwonted radiance to her doll-like face.

"Alison!" she cooed. "How wonderful to see you! Come on in."

I stepped in quietly, not knowing how she'd react to my plea for help. Maybe she'd be flattered; or maybe she'd sense some ulterior motive—a crafty way of getting closer to Randy through his twin. She wasn't stupid by any means—that was exactly why I was coming to her.

She offered me coffee, but I declined. Sitting modestly on the couch, I said: "Andy, I wonder if you could help me."

Her eyes widened, but her general expression remained cautious. She needed to know more about what I wanted.

So I explained. What I needed to have her—or, rather, us— do is to comb the files of the *Dunsmuir Republican* for other incidents at the mine that might be relevant: deaths, accidents, anything that might help to shed light on my father's death. I confess that I was in some ways just as manipulative in dealing with her as I had been with Randy. I frankly played the sympathy card, saying (without in any way alluding to the appalling sight that Randy and I had seen at the grave) that I just needed to come to terms with what had happened to my father. I went on to suggest—what, in fact, I was convinced was true—that my father's fate was not entirely singular. Something like it must have happened before.

Throughout this entire narration, which I gave with a voice that occasionally shook with genuine emotion, Andy gazed at me with that wide-eyed expression, her mouth occasionally opening in a fusion of amazement, sympathetic grief, and puzzlement. Clearly she had not given much thought to the dangers of the mine, even though her own father had had to retire early because of unspecified ailments that had clearly come from his own decades of exhausting work there. And I couldn't help craftily hinting that what we might or might not find through our research might in some dim way help Randy, now that he had already committed years to that dirty and thankless work and could face similar difficulties if we didn't come to his assistance.

At the end of my spiel, all Andy said was, "Okay."

I suspect she welcomed the prospect of getting out of the house. She was not natural housewife material, and I couldn't imagine she was entirely happy puttering around the place all day—there just wasn't enough to do, and she wasn't quite so brainless that she could be satisfied watching soap operas and game shows all afternoon. Anyway, she could justify her working for me by convincing herself that she was really doing it all for Randy's welfare.

So we ambled over to the public library.

I wasn't entirely sure how to proceed. The paper had begun in 1872, about three years after the mine itself had initiated its operations, so we could theoretically get a pretty comprehensive view of the whole history of the mine—or, at least, of any "accidents" or other untoward events that had occurred there—by a systematic reading of the entire run of the paper. I decided to put Andy to the task of reading the more recent issues, starting about fifty years ago. She was no dummy, but probably she would have an easier time digesting news items of this period than those of older vintage, which might be expressed in language she was unfamiliar with.

"But what," she said in her wide-eyed way, "are you looking for?"

"I wish I could tell you, Andy," I said frankly. "Just let me know what you find, and I'll see if it's of any importance."

And so the work began. By the end of that day, I realized that it would take a lot longer than I'd expected. Somehow I thought we could finish in a matter of days, but the paper—especially the older issues, where standards of reporting were very different—was difficult to get through quickly. We couldn't work continuously for hours on end, for our concentration tended to flag after looking at so much newsprint, and we had to take frequent breaks to let our minds rest.

We tended to arrive around 10 A.M., and I would treat Andy to a quick lunch at a greasy-spoon diner a few blocks away before dragging her back to the library to work until about 3 P.M. After one particularly wearying day, I accepted Andy's invitation to stay a while and have some tea and cake before I trudged home.

Andy evidently took some pride in being a hostess, for all that she got very little practice at it: Randy had few friends and didn't seem inclined to invite them over to his house for a meal, and even if he had done so his working-class guests would probably not have been notably impressed by Andy's Emily Post imitation. Maybe she felt that I would be somewhat more appreciative—and I was.

But the tea and cake, instead of reviving me, only made me sleepy. I sat back against the not terribly comfortable couch and closed my eyes for what I thought would be only a few seconds of rest, but then drifted off to sleep.

I was woken in a strange way—by Andy kissing me lightly on the mouth.

My eyes popped open, and I looked at her in astonishment. Andy, sitting next to me on the couch, had a strange light in her eyes, not to mention a furious crimson blush that suffused her entire face.

"What . . . ?" I stammered.

"I'm sorry, Alison!" Andy cried in what seemed like excessive self-abasement. "You just looked so cute sitting there asleep, I couldn't resist!"

"That's all right," I said slowly. And then I reached out and drew her closer to me.

I guess I haven't mentioned that I'm bisexual.

I didn't know I was until I got to college. My two-year involvement with Randy in high school had made me both keen on and wary of entanglements with men, and so I generally kept my distance from the eager young guys at Lehigh who felt they had been liberated from their parents' supervision and could bed down with any girls whom they could cajole into doing so. I didn't get pestered a great deal—my rank as a ravishing vixen wasn't all that high—but there were those who did approach me, and when I rejected them I developed the reputation of being standoffish and even unapproachable. That led to inevitable whispers that I might be a lesbian, and so some actual lesbians began to wonder if they might have a chance with me.

The long and the short of it is that I did in fact plunge into the lesbian subculture on campus. There was something comforting about (a) not having to worry about getting pregnant, and (b) not having to continually soothe the delicate male ego in and out of bed. And I have to say that the first time my bare breasts came into contact with another woman's was an experience not to be missed. *That* was certainly nothing a man could provide!

And yet, I'll be honest and say that I did hunger for the male organ. Lesbian sex is mostly a matter of mutual masturbation—which (don't get me wrong) can be profoundly satisfying, but now and then I yearned for the irreplaceable intimacy of penetration. When the urge became too great, I picked a young man almost at random to fulfill the urge, discarding him almost before he had finished his end of the bargain. That didn't help my reputation any, but by then I was past the point of caring. Just as I knew I'd never have a permanent union with Randy, for all the unending copulation we engaged in, I knew that none of these college boys would make suitable husband material for me.

But what was I, now, to make of Andy's overtures? As we embraced, then kissed, then began fondling each other unabashedly, I sensed that she was in more desperate straits than I was. Here she was, trapped in a weird platonic pseudo-marriage with her own twin brother: there was no possibility of physical intimacy with *him,* but he would probably react with just as much horror and resentment at her establishing any kind of communion with another man—especially another mine worker—as she would if he had taken up with any of the marriageable women in town. They were both caught in a kind of unwelcome but inescapable celibacy—and that's not healthy for anyone.

And so Andy and I drifted over to the bed and did our business. I won't say it was the best lesbian sex I'd ever had, but it was better than adequate. Andy didn't strike me as essentially lesbian anyway: I daresay she longed for a man's caress, but in the absence of that she figured I would do.

You may wonder why I'm going on about my sexual escapades with both Randy and Andy. Surely they are irrelevant to the story I'm telling? I wish they were: it would make this story so much simpler.

We began making our cuddling sessions a regular thing—maybe two or three times a week. At one point Andy frankly asked me if Randy and I were "getting it on," and I had to confess that we'd fooled around a bit. It rather amused me that, for all the relentless intimacy of our high school years, he hadn't yet seen me naked during this summer's shenanigans, but Andy had.

But we continued our work at the library, and we did make some interesting discoveries. The overall picture that emerged, however, seemed to result in greater confusion than before. The upshot was this:

There were any number of incidents that struck us as odd, even tragic and horrific, in spite of the studied blandness with which they were described by the mostly anonymous reporters who covered them. Over the course of more than a century, four or five different patterns could be said to emerge:

1) There were indeed some apparent parallels to what had happened to my father—the deaths of random individuals at or near the mine. No report ever mentioned anything like the burning that my father's body had been subjected to, but that didn't mean it couldn't have happened. A surprising number of these incidents seemed to occur either in spring or in fall (my father had died in the spring of 2016).

2) There were alarming reports, at wide intervals, of miners—or perhaps other individuals associated with the mine—running amok and committing hideous acts of violence. In more than one case, a man killed his entire family, including his baby son, with a hatchet.

3) There were plenty of suicides of miners, at all times of year but possibly more often in spring and fall.

4) There were strange reports of miners—usually veterans who had worked at the mine for twenty years or more—who disappeared, the suggestion being that they had fled to parts unknown. Possibly this was a euphemism for suicide, or perhaps even murder, but what few details the news reports provided suggested an actual departure.

5) There were relatively few deaths that actually and definitively took place at the mine, and these seemed to have been investigated thoroughly and attributed to inadequate safety procedures—which resulted in suitable fines from the Bureau of Mines—or unlucky accidents.

It was difficult to know what to make of these disparate events. The very idea that they could be somehow related, or could have been the result of a single cause or phenomenon, smacked of tinfoil-hat conspiracy theory. And yet, the sheer number of cases—deaths, near-deaths, disappearances, and so on—seemed to preclude the possibility that they were entirely *un*related. But what could possibly be the unifying thread that linked them together, however tenuously?

I had Andy dutifully jot down the relevant details of all the incidents she identified, and then set about following some of them up. Initial results were a spectacular failure.

I attempted to call the surviving relatives of some of the dead miners, but those who didn't simply hang up on me once they sensed the direction of my inquiries proved to be so incredibly equivocal in their grudging elaboration of the event in question that they provided no clarity at all. I distinctly recall one harried widow who, before she slammed the phone down, almost shrieked: "You'd better watch it, missy—you don't know what the hell you're getting into!"

And so I turned my attention back to Randy. It was now he who would have to carry the load, or at least help me carry the load, if I wished to worm out the truth about what had happened to my father—and what was really going on at the Brashear mine.

7

Naturally, he was resistant.

What I felt I now had to do was to approach someone in person—not in a threatening way, but with a certain quiet determination, making a plea that I needed to understand my father's death so I could gain a certain peace of mind and move on with my life. Randy's role would certainly not be that of any kind of strongman, but a fellow miner toward whom the person in question might feel some vicarious sympathy. I was not proud in seizing upon a woman as my first victim: the notion that I could manipulate her feelings more easily than I could a man's (for I didn't think that my seductive wiles could come into play in this scenario) struck me as dismayingly stereotypical, even if true.

I had latched on to a woman whose husband had attempted to kill her three years ago for no ascertainable reason. She was one Miriam Hotchkiss, and she had managed to survive the attack—a knife-thrust to the belly that had resulted in a significant loss of blood but did not prove fatal. Her husband, meanwhile, apparently not caring whether he had completed the execution of his wife, had drawn the bloody knife across his own throat, his blood mingling with hers as he poured out his life in his own living room.

Miriam had subsequently moved—as the online white pages informed me—to a suburb of Elmira, New York. The route there would be fairly direct—I-81 to I-86—and I earmarked the following Saturday for the trip. When I proposed it to Randy, he at once began to whine.

"Oh, gosh, Ali, why do I have to go?"

It was exactly at such moments that he sounded like a ten-year-old boy something I might have found charming at one time, but which now just annoyed me.

"Randy," I said in my best schoolmarm voice, "I need your support—moral and otherwise. You're a miner, and this woman's husband was a miner—at least I think he was. That'll mean a lot to her—perhaps more than the fact that my dad might have worked side by side with her man."

"Maybe she'll talk more freely to one one-on-one—you know, woman to woman."

The comment was surprisingly shrewd. "Maybe," I said, "but I still think it would help if you came along. If she decides she wants a private discussion with me—assuming I can get her to talk at all—then you can take a walk around the block."

Randy eventually gave way with very bad grace. I think part of his reluctance was the fact that the trip, which would probably take only a few hours, wouldn't be nearly long enough—unless by some miracle Miriam had far more information to report than I expected—to warrant an overnight stay at a motel, with attendant snuggling. But I managed to convey, while preserving at least a shred of personal dignity, that I'd make the trip worthwhile somehow and somewhere.

So we made the trip. I'd managed to get both a street address and a phone number (presumably a landline) from the online white pages, and I figured that would be enough. The drive was uneventful, and as we pulled off I-86 (the Southern Tier Expressway) onto Route 352, then south to Route 14, our destination hove into view—the small town of Southport. It was little more than a main street (Penna Avenue) with some streets branching off of it, so it wasn't hard to find the street and the house where Miriam Hotchkiss lived.

It was, I have to say, not the most impressive of homes—but what should I have expected? My own house in Dunsmuir couldn't exactly be considered palatial, and even on the assumption that the magnanimous Conrad Brashear had provided some kind of lump-sum payment—or perhaps even an annuity—to allow Mrs. Hotchkiss to live the rest of her days in modest comfort, this house seemed tired, run-down, *depressed* in some nameless fashion. Its dull gray-blue paint was peeling; the yard was unkempt and needed mowing; there had been no attempt to maintain a garden; and the car parked in the driveway seemed anomalously hunched over, as if embarrassed to be associated with such a dismal residence. No doubt I was reading my own unease into the surroundings, but I now wondered whether this mission would accomplish anything useful aside from a recrudescence of all the pain that she and I felt as a grieving wife and daughter.

And the woman who answered my timid knock fulfilled every expectation I had of what she would look like. She seemed in her early fifties, with wispy gray hair floating untidily around her head like a cloud of gloom. Perhaps she had been attractive once, but whatever curves there might once have been on her stocky frame had now melted into a kind of amorphous mass mercifully hidden by the not entirely clean housedress she wore. Her face seemed to wear an expression of permanent sorrow infused with a kind of tepid resentment.

"Are you Mrs. Hotchkiss?" I said tentatively as she stood before me, gazing at me with dead eyes.

"Yes," she said wearily.

I swallowed hard before proceeding. "You don't know me, but my father worked at the Brashear mine. I wonder—"

At the very mention of the name, she stiffened, and a blaze of fury—and, I could swear, terror—suddenly illuminated her eyes. She started to close the door, but I boldly put my foot in the doorway to prevent her from doing so.

"Please, Mrs. Hotchkiss," I said, "I'd really like to talk to you."

She was deciding how much effort it would take to kick my foot out of the doorway so that she could resume the act of slamming the door in my face. Then she gave a quick glance at Randy, standing irresolutely behind me, perhaps wondering if he might intercede in some violent manner.

"I think you'd better leave," she said tightly.

"I'd just like to talk to you for a few minutes," I pleaded.

"I have nothing to say."

She now did try to move my foot out of the doorway, although her efforts were pretty ineffectual. Like so many people, male and female, she was so unused to physical confrontation that she felt vaguely embarrassed by it even when the need arose.

"Mrs. Hotchkiss," I cried, as she continued to nudge my foot with her own (her efforts were not helped by the fact that she was wearing soft slippers), "my father died in the mine and I need to know why!"

There: I had played my trump card, such as it was. It did have the effect of stopping her in her tracks, however momentarily. As she peered at me her mouth worked, as if she wanted to say something but couldn't decide how best to word it. Then she extended an arm: at first I thought she was now going to resort to pushing me in the chest to thrust me out of her doorway, but in fact she reached up and stroked my face with ineffable gentleness.

"I'm so sorry, dear," she said, eyes rapidly filling with tears, "but you don't want to pursue this."

"Why not?" I cried petulantly.

"You just don't," she said, eyes dropping from mine.

"Can't you tell me anything?"

"It won't help," she said, sounding immensely fatigued. Then she added, oddly: "There's nothing you can do."

I didn't know what to say to that, so we just stood there in a strange face-off.

At last Miriam relented, drawing back so abruptly that I almost tumbled into her house. She released her hold on the door and retreated to what was presumably her living room. She made no explicit invitation for us to enter, but both Randy and I followed her slumped shoulders into a room that was larger than I would have guessed from the outside, and decorated not at all badly, albeit inexpensively.

With only the most infinitesimal gesture of her head, Miriam urged us to sit on the floral sofa positioned against one wall of the room. She didn't take the trouble to offer us refreshments, but merely sat in an easy chair somewhat stiffly, as if girding herself emotionally for an unpleasant interrogation.

As she said nothing but merely stared intently at me, I assumed it was my place to start the inquisition. I offered token sympathy by saying, "I'm very sorry about what happened to you. It's wonderful that you survived."

Her lips curled into a mild sneer. "That's about all I've done—survived."

It was not an auspicious beginning, but I forged ahead. "Do you—do you have any idea why your husband . . . did what he did?"

"No," she said crisply.

"None at all?" I said, my words taking on the urgency of a plea.

She sighed heavily. "How can one ever explain such things? I thought he loved me. In fact"—and she suddenly looked away, then continued as if speaking largely to herself—"perhaps he did even at the end."

"What does that mean?" I cried. "He tried to kill you!"

She looked at me as if I were a child who couldn't possibly understand the workings of the adult world. "My dear, he had been . . . declining for months, maybe years. His behavior had become increasingly erratic. Oftentimes I would find him muttering to himself, or rubbing his hands compulsively as if they were covered in filth that he could never remove. He was—"

"Well," I heedlessly interrupted, "mining is a dirty profession. Randy here can tell you that—he works there." And I gestured in his direction, as if he were some object I had brought to school for show-and-tell.

Miriam gazed at us with a blank expression for what seemed like minutes. Then she said, "My husband didn't work at the mine."

I was thunderstruck.

"But—but—" I stammered. "Then what did he do? Was he an overseer, a supervisor? Was he in administration?" It was pathetically obvious that I was grasping at straws.

Miriam drew herself up with whatever dignity she could summon and said regally, "My husband, Andrew Hotchkiss, was a chemist with a Ph.D. from Columbia University."

"A *chemist!*" I almost shouted. "What on earth would a chemist be doing at a mine?" I wondered if it would have made any difference if I had said that I was a chemist—at least a nascent one—myself.

At once Miriam became cagey, even sly. Her eyes darted around the room as if looking for some sort of distraction or interruption of the trend of the conversation. As I continued to stare fixedly at her, she said unhelpfully, "He—he just was. I thought you knew."

"Knew what?" Only now did I recall that the newspaper article on Hotchkiss's death hadn't specified his occupation.

She abruptly rose from her seat. "I'd really better not say any more. You'll have to figure it out for yourself."

"But how—?" I said, baffled and frustrated. "Figure out *what* for myself?"

"You'd better go," she said, giving me a steely and frankly hostile look. A similar glance at Randy made him retreat into himself as if he'd been chastised by a stern aunt.

I knew we wouldn't get anything more out of Miriam Hotchkiss. Without a word we trudged out of her house and back to our car.

Interchapter 2: October 17, 1938

"I've been chosen," Peter Miller said heavily.

His wife, Flora, turned deathly pale. "Oh, no, Peter, not you!"

"Yes, me."

Both of them knew that this eventuality was a near-certainty; he was a twenty-five-year veteran of the Brashear Mine, and there were few who had worked longer than he had. His two children, a boy and a girl, were grown, and the boy had luckily found employment in Fenton: at least he would be spared such a conversation with his wife when he was only in middle age.

"Wh-what are you going to do?" Flora stammered, wringing her hands.

"What else can I do?" Peter said without looking at her.

"You could—you could run away," she said desperately.

"That would be the act of a coward," he said, a sneer of distaste distorting his mouth. "I know of guys who have done that, but no one has anything good to say about them. And anyway, if that happens Mr. Brashear won't help you."

"We don't need his help!" she cried, the tears now cascading down her face. "We could go away, start afresh somewhere else. At least—"

"Flora," he said, sudden world-weariness descending upon him, "I think it's my time. I'm so tired. I don't have much left in me."

"But what about *me?*" she wailed. "What am *I* supposed to do? Have you given any thought to that?"

"You'll be well provided for. You know that."

"Do you really think that's all I want?" she whispered.

Peter didn't answer. All he said was: "I don't have a choice."

"Of course you do!" she all but spat at him. "You could—"

"I don't have a choice." He got up from the kitchen table and headed to the bedroom to change out of his work clothes. "My mind is made up."

As he walked away from her, a flurry of tremors overtook Flora. She wondered absently if she was about to faint. In a few minutes she managed to get a grip on herself and began fixing dinner, as she had done every day for the past two decades or more.

8

I allowed Randy access to my body at a fairly remote and unfrequented rest stop along I-86 on the drive back home. In spite of the fact that he had been worse than useless in the encounter with Mrs. Hotchkiss, I knew that I had to reward him for his mere presence—not just on this trip, but on a further expedition that I was already contemplating for that very evening. We parked as far away from the other cars as possible, although it was abundantly clear that the other drivers and their passengers were more intent on relieving themselves or stocking up on junk food from the numerous vending machines than on acting as peeping Toms to a pair of oversexed twentysomethings.

Once Randy had satisfied himself, I was all business. Briskly putting my jeans back on and scarcely waiting for him to emerge from the back seat and dump himself into the front passenger seat, I gave him the same sharp look that Miriam had bestowed upon him, saying, "There's a lab at the mine."

Randy just gaped at me—both out of perplexity and out of apprehension that he was being led around like a recalcitrant ox by the women in his life. "I didn't know," he muttered into the hands in his lap.

"I'm not saying you did," I said tartly. "But we have to find it. Now. Maybe tonight."

"Tonight?" he all but squealed. "What if someone's there?"

"Do you know if anyone works at the mine—or anywhere near it—on weekends?"

"Of course not," he said dismissively. "I never go there then. Why the fuck should I?"

His profanity was a feeble attempt to gain control of the situation, but it didn't work. "Well," I said with quiet resolve, "*we're* going there. So I guess we'll find out, won't we?"

Randy sank into his usual sullen silence, saying virtually nothing to me on the remainder of the ride home. Only a few minutes ago he had slaked his appetite for my flesh—and now I was going to jeopardize his job, and perhaps even his life, just to satisfy some perverse curiosity of my own. *What is it about women?* I'm sure he was whining to himself.

I dropped him off at his house and returned to my own. I certainly wasn't planning on having dinner with him; and anyway, any unauthorized invasion of the mine had to be done pretty late at night, on the assumption that this lab—which I now knew had to exist—might in fact be functioning during the evenings and/or weekends. The very fact that a miner of several years' standing like Randy didn't know of its existence suggested that there was, at a minimum, something covert about it. Whether there was anything actually criminal—and, more to the point, whether and why my father might have been involved in it, were questions I was not entirely certain I could answer in a single foray. But I had to start somewhere.

So at 1 A.M. that night I pulled up to Randy's house and waited patiently. There was no particular need to keep this excursion secret from Andy, but there was likewise no compelling need for her to know of it. Whether Randy had told her was not of the slightest concern to me: what, indeed, could she do? Notify the authorities? What would that accomplish except get her own twin brother into needless trouble?

Randy sidled out of his front door several minutes after I had arrived—his delay constituting, in my judgment, another silly gesture of rebellion against the plan and against me personally. But I made no reaction when he entered my vehicle, and I simply drove off without a word in the direction of the mine.

Everyone knew that the main entrance to the mine proper was on the far eastern end—and I recalled that that newspaper article announcing my father's death had mentioned a previously unknown (to me, at least) western entrance. That was obviously the place to begin.

But the mine covered an immense amount of territory, and it was girded by a barbed-wire fence around its entire circumference, precisely to prohibit intruders such as myself. I had to park at quite a distance from the putative western entrance, whose exact location I could only guess at. I had brought only a flashlight with me, for I couldn't imagine what else would be of any use. The idea of having a gun struck me as preposterous. Even if someone were there, I wasn't about to go blasting my way into the mine's (or the lab's) inner precincts. This current mission was exploratory only.

We had to make our way through a dense, tree-choked acclivity in approaching the western end of the mine, and when that barbed-wire fence loomed above us—at least ten feet in height—we found ourselves intimidated by it. At least it wasn't electrified, as a quick probing of it with a dry stick established.

But there was more than the fence to send a chill through us. Only some fifty feet from us—and from what I took to be some kind of opening or entrance—was an armed guard.

This fellow had a shotgun draped casually over his shoulder, and in all honesty he looked rather bored by his seemingly useless task. I, of course, was dumbfounded by the man's very presence: what could possibly be so vital that such a person was required in the very midst of a sleepy summer weekend? I suppose I should not have assumed anything overtly or potentially illegal: a shrewd businessman like Conrad Brashear might simply have been taking extra care in guarding company secrets. But somehow I couldn't bring myself to believe that.

The man was not stationary, but every so often got up and wandered about the general area, sometimes entirely out of our vision. After nearly an hour watching him carefully, I began to sense a pattern to his actions and felt that an opportunity to flit through that entrance might present itself if we timed our invasion carefully. And so I said to Randy:

"Okay, we're going over."

I'm not sure I was any more spry at climbing than Randy was, but my desire to avoid pain made me exceptionally careful as I ascended that fence. The most fruitful course, it seemed to me, was to climb as close as possible to one of the tall wooden poles that anchored the fence every twenty feet or so—and so it proved to be. I attained the top of the fence without incident, but when I looked down I saw Randy merely gazing up at me with a blank look of terror. I gestured firmly, even a bit frantically, with my head and arms for him to follow suit, but he refused to do so until I had gingerly crossed over the top of the fence—catching the sleeve of my blouse at one point on the barbed wire but quickly extricating it—and come all the way down to the ground on the other side. Only then—and only after I gave him a malign glare through the barbed wire—did he grudgingly follow. A hiss of breath led me to suspect that he hadn't been quite as careful as I, and sure enough he was sucking the back of his hand as red drops emerged from a smallish wound there.

We had to wait a good many minutes, lying flat on our stomachs, before the guard went around a bend and out of view. At that point I leaped up and raced toward the entrance, Randy following with a muffled cry only, it seemed, out of fear of being left alone.

We slipped into the entrance undetected.

What confronted us was a long, concrete-lined corridor that seemed to be relatively level—that is, it wasn't descending into the bowels of the earth and therefore into the mine proper. At the very end of the corridor was a heavy-looking steel door. I gingerly tried to knob—it was locked.

Randy, who I could see was sweating profusely in spite of the cool night air, seemed to collapse in defeat. He had followed my reckless infiltration into an obviously forbidden section of the mine, only to be stymied on the verge of revelation. He was already starting to skulk back in the direction of the entrance when I touched his arm, silently urging him to stay put.

I took out a nail file from my pocket.

There's no need to explain how I had gained the knowledge to pick a lock—at least, certain relatively easy ones. And I had no idea whether this lock would be of such a type: why should it, given that the very existence of this entire area was so manifestly a secret? And yet, the lock in fact gave way to my careful and patient efforts. The process takes far longer than it does in the movies, and I was at it a full fifteen minutes. More sweat was pouring from Randy's face; its sharp tang and the stains appearing all over his plain work shirt made it abundantly evident that he was just about jumping out of his skin in an agony of impatience and anticipatory guilt. His frenetic "Hurry up, Ali!" at one point didn't help matters, and I gave him a withering glance and told him to bide his time.

But I was successful in the end. Those fifteen minutes may have seemed like hours or days, but they were necessary for me to gain a feel for the kind of lock I was dealing with, so that I could take action accordingly. A satisfying, but disturbingly loud, click—which in fact made Randy leap back as if electrocuted—revealed that I had succeeded.

I turned the knob and entered, leaving Randy to shuffle in after me.

Closing the door, I felt it was safe enough to turn on the overhead light whose switch I found on the left-hand wall as I entered. What faced me when the light came on was something I could not quite grasp.

It was a lab—an immense one. The room must have been at least fifty feet square, perhaps seventy. The number of desks full of highly advanced chemical machinery was similarly vast. I could easily see twenty chemists working here without encumbrance. Quite literally every table had state-of-the-art gas masks lying carelessly around, and against one wall were dozens of hazmat suits that would cover one's frame from head to toe. On another wall was a huge bank of what looked like industrial-sized freezers, humming with quiet insistence. Over in a corner I noted some ominous-looking large barrels or tubs clearly marked as radioactive waste.

A B.S. in chemistry doesn't in any way guarantee that I know everything there is to know about the subject, but somehow this bewildering place caused me to experience some sort of mind-freeze. How could the mine possibly be radioactive? Could that somehow account for the anomalous number of deaths—not only of mine workers (and others, as in the case of the chemist Andrew Hotchkiss) but also, in a few tragic cases, their loved ones? If so, how could the mine keep operating at all? Surely the Bureau of Mines or the EPA or some other state or federal agency would have shut the mine down years or decades ago. Or was it that this phase of the mine activity was done in such absolute secrecy that none of the supervising agencies had any knowledge of the matter?

Then there was the quandary of what my father's involvement in all this was. He was a miner, pure and simple; his knowledge of chemistry was probably poorer than the average high school student's. Could he have been somehow assigned as one of the late-night guards, like the one whose patrol we had so easily evaded? But why would the mine operators have designated him for such a position, for which he also had little training? And even if that had happened, I was no closer to explaining how and why he had died. Did he poke his nose into something he shouldn't have? As a result, was his death more along the lines of a murder—or even an execution? Who was responsible, in that case? And why would the culprits have felt the need to *burn* his body, to say nothing of bearing off his skull to parts unknown? Why not just slit his throat and be done with it?

As Randy was wandering around the lab in a daze of wide-eyed confusion, my own attention suddenly shifted to a curious contrivance at the very back of the lab. It seemed to me, at this distance, to be a kind of conveyor belt; but as I approached it more closely, I saw that there was actually no belt that would move material along. Instead, it was simply a long, low metal platform with a raised edge on either side where objects could be placed—for what reason, I could not begin to fathom. The platform covered the entire length of the back wall, and at one end of it there was what looked like a door, roughly three feet square, made of solid wrought-iron, with a heavy handle in its direct center.

Only now did I realize that there was a different kind of humming or throbbing—different from that of the freezers on the wall to the right of the door. The closest analogy I can make is to an immense sloshing, as of a tidal wave running up against an insurmountable barrier. But the substance that was making the sloshing noise seemed much thicker than water—more like some inconceivably titanic quantity of gelatin.

What instinct of folly or madness led me to try to open that door, I will never know. I was already faced with an abundance of evidence that radioactive material was present somewhere in the vicinity—and yet, here I was, proposing to unleash whatever lay beyond that wrought-iron door, without protection of any kind.

But my first attempts to open that door were frustrated: I pulled and tugged in every direction, but it refused to budge. I wondered if there was some lock on it, but I could not readily see anything of the kind. By accident I realized that the way to open the door was not to pull but to *lift*—that is, lift straight up.

As I did so, something immediately poured out of the aperture I had exposed.

It is hard for me, even now, to describe my initial impressions upon seeing this material. Even its color was indefinable: initially I thought it was white, but it would be more accurate to say that it was translucent, with a myriad of multicolored particles within its essence, all moving or flitting in some perplexing fashion and so rapidly that the eye quickly tired of watching any single particle or even the collocation of all the particles. My overall belief—for I at least retained the residual sense not to touch the thing—was that it was thick and viscous, for it expanded and contracted in a slow, glutinous fashion as it poured out of the aperture, running along the motionless "conveyor belt" in front of me. Every now and then a bubble would form somewhere on its surface and then pop nervously, emitting a curious odor—not unpleasant, but merely inscrutable.

I was startled into inaction when I first saw this blob or

mass moving briskly along the platform; and it was some seconds before I recognized that I had the power to halt its seemingly unconscious or autonomic action. I could simply release the door, which I had continued to hold in the midst of my horror and amazement.

Only then did I grasp a vital point about that door: its lower edge was razor-sharp, in the manner of a guillotine.

As a result, the door neatly sliced off a large piece of the viscous entity that was continuing to poor onto the platform. The moment it did so, a hideous roar filled the place—exactly the sort of groan or moan that I had heard periodically throughout the years I had spent in this town.

At that sound—which, for all that I have used such loaded terms to describe it, was not to my mind unequivocally produced by a living creature—Randy turned to me and gasped loudly, crying, "Ali, what have you done?" I could immediately tell that he had recognized the sound also, although he knew as little as I did what to make of it.

We didn't have much time to reflect on any of this, for along the long corridor that led to this lab I could hear thunderous footsteps and a harsh voice saying, "Hey! Who's in there?"

Well, now we were in for it. Glancing frantically around the large room, I could not at once detect any means of egress except for the door by which we had entered—a door that was already being blocked by the lanky guard now bursting through it. When the guard caught sight of us, he seemed as astounded as we were—but he wasted no time in raising his rifle to his shoulder and firing at us.

Once again, this is not the way it is in the movies. For me, anyway, the spectacle of being fired upon with a high-caliber weapon by a person who has shown not the slightest inclination to determine our purpose in being here was so petrifying that time seemed to stand still. Mercifully, the bullet aimed at me went wide, for I was still almost fifty feet from my assailant, and his own agitation rendered his aim poor at best. The shot rang noisily off the concrete wall behind me, less than a foot from my head. Randy, who was in the middle of the room and had seen the guard rush in, merely ducked under a metal table for transient protection. I did the same, which compelled the guard to enter more boldly into the room and stalk us, one at a time, in what was obviously an unquestioned mission to obliterate us from the earth. He first turned his attention to Randy, who was marginally closer to him than I was; and as he bolted around the corner of the table where he suspected Randy to be, he raised his gun again to his shoulder and pointed it downward. A shot rang out, and I heard Randy emit a harsh grunt. I feared the worst, but then realized that his cry was only one of adrenaline-filled surprise; the shot had missed him, if only by inches, as he scuttled around another table.

I now wondered whether we might be able to outmaneuver the guard by continually shuffling around the tables and then exiting the room; but the prospect seemed remote, and there was a strong likelihood that at least one of us would be felled by the man's repeated shooting. Then, in a corner of the room not far from the door, I saw what I felt, in my desperation, was our only chance of escape—an elevator.

As I scooted on hands and knees toward it, I actually passed Randy, who was struggling to get a grip on himself after being fired upon. His eyes were wide and rather crazed, and he seemed to be trembling throughout his entire frame. I hissed, "Over there!" pointing to the elevator. It took him a moment or two to figure out what I had in mind, but then realization dawned and he followed me, slinking along the floor like an injured animal. I pressed the button on the wall, and to my amazement the elevator opened at once. We plunged in, and I punched a random button on the inside wall just to get the door to close.

The guard now sensed that he had been bamboozled, and with an enraged cry, "Hey, you fuckers!" he once again aimed his shotgun at us. The bullet pinged off the closing door of the elevator, but that was all.

As I heard the guard pounding the now closed door in frustrated fury, I became aware that we were heading in a downward direction—the only direction, indeed, the elevator went from the floor we had been on. There were at least four levels where the elevator theoretically stopped, and we were heading for the lowest one.

I had no idea of the contours of the mine at this point, and I wondered if even Randy would be of any help in what seemed the insurmountable task of escaping from it without further detection. As we sat on the floor of the elevator, breathing stertorously and covered in sweat, we merely gazed at each other. I don't doubt that he was cursing me inwardly for getting him into this unprecedented mess, but I sensed that beyond this emotion was a dim awareness of some highly anomalous goings-on here that had been kept from him and the other miners. To that extent he was coming to see that some inexplicable injury or injustice had been done to him also. I didn't know how much of the viscous entity he had actually seen, but that groan or roar was still haunting his mind.

As for me, I was no closer to a resolution of my core concern—what, in fact, had happened to my father?—than I was before; but I too sensed that there was something very wrong with this whole situation. My father's fate was now only a small part of an overriding concern with the fates of all the men who had toiled away at this place for a hundred years or more, a few of them dying in some spectacular and incomprehensible fashion but the great majority giving their entire lives to an operation that may have been merely a sham or cover for something far different, and far more sinister.

But those questions would have to wait. As the elevator door opened briskly at the fourth underground level, we exited on tenterhooks, not knowing what we would find facing us. I alertly took precautions against immediate pursuit by quickly locating a sturdy piece of wood and placing it in the path of the elevator door, preventing it from closing and therefore preventing the guard—or anyone else—on the main floor from using the elevator to come after us. No doubt there were other means of reaching this level, but presumably they would be more difficult and time-consuming.

It was obvious, from Randy's baffled and harried looks as he canvassed the area where we found ourselves, that he hadn't the faintest idea where we were or that this whole section of the mine existed. We were clearly well to the west of the central mine shaft; but for my part, I was not entirely certain I even wished to head in that direction, for who knew what guards might be positioned there? Indeed, the chances of our escaping from this place, in whatever direction, seemed risibly meager, to the point that I almost wished to collapse and give up right now, in spite of our momentary reprieve from capture.

We were in a long, barren corridor that snaked off in both directions from the elevator, and it was not immediately apparent which way we should go. Detecting what appeared to be a faint glow in the far distance along the path to our left, I urged Randy to proceed there. The glow could not possibly represent daylight, of course; but in the pitch blackness in which we found ourselves, any illumination, however dim and however problematical its source, seemed somehow reassuring.

So we began trotting to our left. At some point the walls ceased to be of finished concrete and became merely a conglomeration of hard-packed dirt and ragged veins of coal: this section of the corridor had clearly been hewed out of the solid ground, for what purpose we could scarcely fathom. I was not encouraged by the rhythmical sloshing sound that seemed to emanate behind the wall to our left—that is, the inner wall of the corridor—but tried for the nonce to put that out of my mind.

We saw crudely constructed staircases heading down at various points, but it would surely have been folly to descend even further into the bowels of the earth. Why there were no staircases leading up was more than a little perplexing: was that elevator the only means to ascend? If so, our fates were sealed.

But now, another sound suggested that they were sealed in any case.

A succession of clopping footsteps—almost as if from the shod shoes of a horse, but surely from a posse of jackbooted guards—could be heard emanating mechanically behind us. We redoubled our pace, although it was not at all certain that the way forward was any more likely to lead to our emergence from this underground nightmare than the way behind. That light had minimally increased in potency—but so had the sloshing. Both of us became almost paralyzed with indecision, dreading capture—or death—from the pursuing guards but petrified at whatever was causing that pale, sick-looking glow. Whatever Randy had or had not seen, I myself could not forget the loathsome entity back in that cryptic laboratory.

Without warning, the corridor—at times so narrow that we had difficulty running together side by side—suddenly veered to the right and opened wide, to an almost infinite extent; and what's more, the wall of dirt and coal gave way to an incalculably vast barrier of clear glass. What faced us on the other side of that glass was such as to beggar our imaginations.

It was the originator of that sickly light. It was the entity—creature—thing—whose minuscule appendage I had unwittingly hacked off. Reaching dozens, hundreds of feet above our heads—and, in all likelihood, just as much below our feet—was a mass of white or translucent jelly, sprinkled with shimmering dark pellets within its depths, moving with incandescent life like an innumerable array of electrons circling the nucleus in the classic but misleading image of the atom. The creature—if indeed it was one single entity—was rolling and bubbling and folding and creasing in an exquisitely slow and curiously stately dance; parts of it would expand and contract at random, while other parts would shoot off temporary fragments of itself in what little space there was to do so—but these parts would quickly return to the main body of the thing, as if unwilling to part from its apparent source for even a moment.

It had no coherent shape; nothing that could be described as arms, legs, torso, head, or back. The mere attempt to liken it to anything terrestrial was doomed to futility. I am aware that the earth holds many strange things within itself, whether it be in the remote reaches of the untenanted wilderness or in the inky depths of the sea; but I instinctively sensed that this entity was in no way earthly, and that its purpose, motivations, and very existence were beyond the comprehension of our little minds.

But, somewhat mercifully, I did not have much time to ponder on this creature's nature and properties; for in both directions we were suddenly beset by gun-toting guards, one of whom swiftly knocked Randy out with a derisive thrust of his pistol while another bestowed upon me the same gift of unconsciousness.

9

I awoke groggily in what I assumed was a hospital bed; but almost as soon as I partially shook the cobwebs from my mind I understood that this was no ordinary hospital, or perhaps not a hospital at all. In fact, I was lying on an almost excessively soft four-poster canopied bed, with thick and expensive blankets covering me almost to suffocation. Through the gauze of the canopy I saw a nondescript-looking woman of indeterminate age dressed in a white nurse's uniform; but when I groaned in pain and felt the large lump on the back of my head, this woman made only the most token effort to take stock of my condition before she blandly turned on her heels and left the room.

In a matter of moments she had returned, accompanied by a man much taller than herself. Even through the canopy I could see that this person was bald as a cue ball and dressed in a peculiar kind of suit or uniform that struck me as something from the future. As the nurse parted the gauze curtain, the man looked down at me as if scrutinizing a moderately interesting insect, then nodded to himself and walked away.

The nurse now did take the trouble to tend to my needs, checking that lump on my head, taking my temperature, and urging me to drink some orange juice she handed me. I managed to get it down, and it revived my spirits more than I could have imagined.

"Can you get up?" the nurse bluntly asked.

Without replying, I tried to do just that—but a wave of

nausea and light-headedness overcame me, and I actually fell against her chest and clung to her like a child. She seemed inclined to put me back into bed, but I gritted my teeth and managed to get to my feet, although I still needed to hold on to the nurse's shoulders.

She led me out through one of the several doors in the room, and I saw that I was in an office of sorts—but one so immense that I had difficulty taking in the contours and parameters of the place. I could see that one wall was lined with books, while other walls featured shelving that bore some choice objets d'art juxtaposed incongruously with high-tech electronic equipment of various kinds.

The nurse led me to a squarish desk that, although of moderate size, was nonetheless so dwarfed by the gargantuan room that it seemed like a toy. It had next to nothing on it aside from a gold pen in a holder, a telephone, and a small array of family photos.

The person seated at the desk was the man who had peeked into my room a few moments before. Aside from his perfect baldness, he was slender almost to gauntness, but with a suggestion of wiry toughness that made him a quietly formidable figure. The suit or costume he wore was such as to suggest a person from the future. He was probably in his early forties, but the intense blue of his piercing eyes and the lively alertness of his sharp features made him seem younger.

I did not need to be introduced to him to know his identity; his picture had appeared in the local paper often enough during my childhood and adolescence. Apparently out of formality, however, he did introduce himself, extending a hand.

"I am glad you are well, Miss Mannering," he said in a rich baritone voice that exuded commanding authority. "I am Conrad Brashear."

I felt it would be needlessly impolite not to take the hand, so I did so. But I did remark sourly: "I wouldn't say I'm well. Your goon gave me quite a blow to the back of my head."

"I'm sorry about that," Brashear said, actually sounding sincere. "But you and your friend did enter an unauthorized area."

I wasn't going to argue the point. "I know that," I said tartly. "I was trying to get to the bottom of—of what happened to my father. He was Guy Mannering, and he—"

"I know who he was," Brashear interrupted briskly. "And I know of your interest in his—fate."

"You do?" I said, although I was not surprised at his words. "Then maybe you can explain why—why his body . . ." I choked on the words. Dizziness overcame me for a time, and I came close to passing out.

Brashear looked at me with obvious concern and seemed on the verge of summoning the nurse; but I waved my hand in a curt gesture of dismissal and presently regained my composure.

When he was convinced that I was not going to faint on him like some Victorian neurasthenic, he stared keenly—but not, I will confess, without some latent sympathy—at me, got up from the chair, and began pacing back and forth behind the desk. I sat silent: the ball was in his court, and it was his obligation to respond. Maybe he wouldn't tell me the truth—or at least the whole truth—but he had a moral obligation to say *something*.

"What happened to him," he said slowly, "was unfortunate."

A sudden insight flashed through my mind. "But it was no 'accident'?" I said accusingly.

"No," he said, his tone heavy with regret, "it was no accident."

Once again I became dizzy—not from the effect of the blow to my head, but from the immensity of what I sensed to be the anomalies and mysteries confronting me. In a tone that sounded dismayingly close to a whine, I said:

"Please tell me what's going on here."

Again, his gaze seemed a mix of concern—both for himself and for me—and a sort of objective pity. He did not reply immediately: clearly he was choosing his words with monumental care.

"It is difficult to know where to begin," he said.

"Why not try the beginning?" I shot back with cheap sarcasm.

He smiled out of the side of his mouth. "The fact is that no one knows what the beginning *is*. I understand you have been doing quite a bit of research into the history of the mine—"

It was my turn to interrupt him. "Not the mine—just the deaths at the mine, or the deaths of people who worked at or in the vicinity of the mine and the deaths of the family members of those who worked at the mine. Yeah," I concluded viciously, "you could say I've been looking into that."

My words didn't have any appreciable effect on him. If he thought I was going to report these anomalies to some state or federal agency, or perhaps to go the press, he seemed singularly unconcerned. I got a faint sense that he had bigger fish to fry.

Several times he seemed on the verge of speaking, only to lapse into a frustrated silence. So I took the bull by the horns.

"And what of that—that *thing*—I saw? That horrible white thing that you've somehow trapped down there—that creature that may be miles and miles across—"

"Yes, that 'creature,' as you call it," he replied almost whimsically. "That's the core of the matter, isn't it?"

"What *is* it?" I said in an agony of frustration. "Where did it come from? What's it doing down there?"

He gazed at me as if I were a dense undergraduate who had suddenly grasped the theory of relativity in a single intuitive rush.

"What is it?" he said. "I have no idea. Where did it come from? I can only guess. What it's doing down there? That's the simplest question to answer:

"It is eating up all our coal."

I could do nothing but sit silent and gaping.

"Perhaps 'eating' is not quite the right word: it may be a mistake to think that the entity in any way resembles anything human or even terrestrial." This echo of a thought that had coursed through my own mind the moment I had seen the thing startled me into further silence. He went on: "I suppose 'absorbing' is the best way to put it. The creature absorbs the coal—and it grows. That much, and that much only, is clear to me after all these years."

"You're telling me," I said, aghast, "that it's been there for *years?*"

"Years?" he said mockingly. "Perhaps decades. Perhaps a century or more." Turning on his heel so that he looked pensively out the large picture window behind his desk, he said, "I imagine your researches have alerted you to the fact that there was a meteor shower in this general vicinity around 1907."

I confess I had only vaguely paid attention to the scanty news reports of that event in my canvassing of the newspaper, for it didn't seem to have any relevance to what I was looking for.

"Maybe that was the source of the thing, maybe not. All I know is—and this is no doubt something your own researches have determined—that the various deaths and other unfortunate events at or near the mine began to occur a few years later."

Again, I had failed to make the connection. So much for my ability to put two and two together! I remained mute.

"Let us assume that is the case," he went on. "The issue that confronted my ancestors was: what to do about it."

Now I began putting two and two together—and in the

most appalling way. A burning flash of anger and outrage flitted through my entire frame, and when I spoke it was with a tremolo of towering indignation.

"You—your 'ancestors'—sacrificed the men at the mine. Twice a year, in spring and in fall. They were scapegoats: you might as well have slit their throats at May Eve and Hallowmas. The thing—the creature—'absorbed' them, and then regurgitated what it couldn't use or didn't want. It ate my father, and then spit out his bones!"

By the end of my speech I was shouting, perhaps shrieking. But Brashear's response was not what I expected.

With a face suddenly rubicund with outrage of his own—outrage and profound resentment at the injustice of the accusation I had hurled at him—he spat out his words with icy venom.

"Do you think those men were 'sacrificed' to make it grow?" he said, his own voice rising by decibels with each word. *"They were sacrificed to prevent it from growing!"*

I was stunned by his revelation. I was not entirely ready to believe him, but his own fury and conviction had the effect of deflating me.

"I know," he continued with a bitter sneer, "you would dearly love to see me and my forbears as heartless capitalists—petty dictators who relish the thought of consigning their workers to a horrible death to put more money in our pockets. The reality is that we wanted to keep the mine operating as long as possible. We knew that the mine was vital to this town's very existence, and we took very seriously our responsibility in maintaining it as long as it could viably be maintained. None of my ancestors, nor the specialists they quietly called in to examine the situation, could come up with any solution to the difficulty we faced: that creature, which clearly has an affinity for carbon in all its forms, was growing inexorably, even if slowly. Somehow, probably through trial and error, it was discovered that sending living human creatures into the maw of that entity would inhibit its growth, at least for a time. It was the best solution we could come up with."

He sighed heavily and continued speaking in a low monotone.

"A lottery was established, open to those men who had worked for more than twenty years in the mine. The one who was chosen for that season—either spring or fall—was assured that his wife and family would be well provided for upon his death; and they were. It was an open secret among the old-timers, although naturally they didn't let the younger chaps know: their work was hard enough without the prospect of certain death facing them in two decades' time."

At last I found words, after a fashion. "You—you just let these people die?" I said feebly.

Brashear placed both of his hands firmly on the table and stared at me.

"You'd be surprised, Ms. Mannering, how many of the chosen—scapegoats, as you call them—welcomed their fate. Oh, to be sure, some of them ran away and were never heard from again, but the great majority made peace with their selection. Twenty years working in a mine beats a man down—he is ready for a rest. And the rest that instantaneous death provides is often far more desirable than the long, quiet, lingering death of a monotonous retirement with nothing to do and nowhere to go."

I suddenly felt the need to leap up from my seat and pace around the vast office, clenching and unclenching my hands. I spun on my heels just as Brashear had done and spat at him:

"This is horrible and insane and grotesque! You're telling me that you and your cadre of 'specialists' couldn't find a more humane way of—of retarding the growth of this vile creature than plunging your own men down its throat? What about animals? They're living creatures, too, full of carbon. What about that secret laboratory you or your ancestors set up? Are you saying that your crack team of chemists couldn't come up with some formula that would diminish or even kill that thing altogether? What the hell's that lab for anyway?"

I was quite literally huffing and puffing with emotion, and I didn't appreciate Brashear holding up a hand patronizingly as if to calm down a hysterical female.

"So many questions," he said snidely, "and so many answers that will not please you. I doubt whether sending animals down into the belly of that creature would have been very much more humane than sending men, but for some reason that didn't work—or at least not so well. There are records indicating that someone decades ago tried offering the thing a bear. It was no go. Yes, the bear died, but otherwise it was rejected by the entity in no uncertain terms.

"As for that laboratory—" Brashear sighed heavily again. "It is not nearly as nefarious as you seem to think. I know of your background in chemistry, so I'm surprised you haven't deduced its function. The fact of the matter is that, through sheer accident, my father determined about thirty years ago that the creature could be made to yield certain valuable materials, albeit through a highly time-consuming and laborious process.

"In short," he said with a certain smug satisfaction, "we began extracting rare earth metals out of the entity."

I was stupefied. Maybe I should have been able to figure that out on my own—but I had other things on my mind when I was exploring that lab.

"I won't bore you with the details of the procedure. But I will say that this discovery was a godsend not just to me and my family, but to the miners themselves. Surely you must know that mining is in fairly dire straits—as an industry it is dying, with no chance of resurrection. Cheap natural gas, and now cheap renewables, are consigning coal quite literally to the dustbin of history. But the fact that we can now sell rare earth metals to a worldwide market has allowed me to keep this mine open when, by every sane principle of economics, it should have been closed years ago.

"There is, however, a problem. As I say, the process of extracting the metals from the creature is so enormously difficult that it has certain unfortunate long-term effects on the chemists brought in—secretly, as you so correctly state—to manage the task. Yes, of course they use protective gear of the most comprehensive sort, but that does not seem to help; it only delays the inevitable.

"Their minds get affected somehow—we've never been able to learn how, as we have not had the wherewithal to conduct an autopsy, which would also have to be done in secret. So the result is that on a few occasions the chemists . . . run amok—"

"And try to kill themselves and their families," I finished for him, thinking of Mrs. Hotchkiss.

"Yes," Brashear said heavily.

"And you don't care about that—you just want to get your hands on those metals."

Again he bristled. "The chemists are fully notified as to the dangers of the job—and they are paid very, very well."

"Mrs. Hotchkiss doesn't seem to be in the lap of luxury."

"Who?" he said, momentarily confused. "Oh, her. Well, her husband had contracted some fairly extensive debts—that was why he had come to us in the first place. We offered to pay him far more than he could feasibly have received from any other employer. But of course we couldn't possibly maintain that level of reimbursement after his self-inflicted death."

"No, of course not," I said in weak sarcasm.

Once again he turned his back to me, gazing reflectively out the window.

"I confess, Ms. Mannering, that I am getting a bit fatigued by this discussion. You now know about as much as you are entitled to know—rather more, in my judgment. The question at the end of the day is: What are you now going to do?" He turned quietly to face me.

I was momentarily speechless. This long, bizarre, dreadful tale had drained me of emotion—I felt like a hollow shell. The whole situation seemed so utterly hopeless that for a time I simply wanted to run out of this office and head out, as he himself had said, for "parts unknown"—someplace so far away from Dunsmuir that I would eventually forget its very name, let alone the seething, bubbling entity trapped under the seemingly placid surface of its drab terrain. But of course I knew that that was the most frivolous form of wishful thinking.

"What can I do?" I said wearily. "What can *we* do? That thing is there, growing inch by inch, day by day, and nothing can stop or retard it except the periodic sacrifice of a few good men. What point would there be of reporting any of this to the police, or to state or federal authorities? I could force you to show them that creature—but then what? Drop a nuke on Dunsmuir? That might blast the creature to smithereens."

"Yes, I suppose it might," Brashear said wistfully, as if actually contemplating the prospect for a moment. Snapping out of his reverie, he said almost cheerfully, "I'm glad you've adopted such a sensible attitude. We may be sitting on a powder-keg, but we can at least do all we can to prevent it from blowing up in our faces for as long as we can. Trust me, my dear, the thought weighs upon me every moment of the day and night."

He turned and looked out the window contemplatively. "I am not an evil man. I am simply a man caught in a horrendously untenable situation. If you can think of any alternative to our current course of action, I would welcome it."

"I'll take it under advisement," I said. Then, turning serious: "Just one more question, if you will. I suspect you know that I, um, exhumed my father's remains."

He nodded fractionally.

"Can you tell me why—why there was no skull? Where did it go? Did the—the creature keep or absorb it?"

Brashear closed his eyes, patently reluctant to answer. At last he said: "You may have to ask your mother."

"My *mother?*" I cried. "What the hell does she have to do with all this?"

Once again that heavy sigh. "I have deceived you on one small point: the 'scapegoat' does not, strictly speaking, have to be alive when he is sent down to meet his fate. A recently deceased body, so long as it is quite fresh, would do just as well." Looking at me straight in the face, he went on: "Some men prefer that alternative."

A shiver began coursing through my entire frame, and even as I wrapped my arms around my body I couldn't seem to stop.

"No," I moaned, "no, please don't say . . ."

"I'm sure," Brashear said softly, "that what she did was merciful. But our undertaker, Mr. Knowles, felt it prudent to dispose of the head in the event that some snooper just like yourself might take the initiative to investigate the matter. His action was really rather irrational, for surely the state of the rest of your father's remains would elicit more than a small measure of baffled inquiry. But that was his decision."

I stood up stiffly, uncertain whether I was even capable of leaving that expansive office without collapsing in a heap. I was not about to ask Brashear's permission to leave, and he made no attempt to stop me. Where Randy was, and whether his injuries were worse than mine, were matters I suddenly found utterly inconsequential. All I wanted to do was go home—but the inevitable conversation I would have to have with my mother made me doubt whether that was a destination that would have any meaning for me anymore.

*

She could tell, from my expression as I stumbled through the front door, that I knew.

She was, predictably, puttering in the kitchen, wrapped in a wifely apron. As she stalked into the living room to confront me—I had, after all, been gone an entire night, with no account of my whereabouts—she initially seemed on the verge of giving me a resentful tongue-lashing. But the look she saw on my face made her retreat, almost back to the perceived safety of that kitchen, the domain she had ruled for the better part of three decades.

"Alison," she said, holding out her arms as if to ward off a blow, "you mustn't—"

"How did you do it, Mom?" I said, unutterably weary. "Just tell me how you did it."

She didn't answer that question directly. Now standing firm at the threshold of the kitchen, she released a torrent of words in an angry whine. "He wanted to go, Alison! He wanted to! He was chosen, and he wasn't going to evade his responsibility! He knew it would be for the good of the mine—for the good of the town! He was a good man, he knew what he had to do! It's just that he—"

"Just tell me how, Mom," I repeated. "That's all I want to know. I don't blame you. I don't blame *him.* I'm not saying anything could have been different."

Her glance softened, although it was still wary and apprehensive. Her mouth worked, and she licked lips that had suddenly gone dry. Then she peered at the floor and muttered, "The shotgun, of course. Nothing else would have been certain. I knew how to use that gun. It was all we had. I couldn't possibly have used a knife, and I had no pills I could give him. So it had to be the gun. Just to the back of the head. He sat in a chair in the back yard. It was over in no time. And then Brashear's men came and took him away." Her voice trailed off indecisively.

"Okay," I said, and made my way to my room. I suddenly felt like a child, retreating into the space that Mom and Dad had bestowed upon me for my personal use—a fleeting haven from the horrors of the world, and from my parents' own importunities. I closed the door, locked it, and fell onto the bed.

Then I slept like the dead.

10

It was on the following Saturday evening that I felt the earth tremor.

My mother and I had just concluded another heavy meal, only a fraction of which I could stuff into my mouth. We said virtually nothing to each other, and what we did say consisted of only the most inconsequential mundanities. It would be something of an understatement to say that my knowledge of my mom's murder of my dad—a mercy killing, if you wished to be charitable about it—had permanently affected my relationship with her. In fact, even in the three days that had passed since I learned the appalling truth, I was unable to assimilate the information in any coherent way. There she was, looking as doughy and mildly resentful as she always did: the idea that this harmless-looking woman could have blasted my father's head off was simply not comprehensible. And the fact that this single tragedy was a kind of metonymy for the vast, engulfing horror and tragedy that lay beneath our very feet made it that much harder to grasp.

And so I did what we are all tempted to do in such situations: I pretended that nothing had really happened, nothing had really changed.

In all honesty, all I wanted to do was to get out of this place. The renewal of my relations with Randy—and my unexpected physical involvement with Andy—had not only failed to tie my heart and mind to my birthplace, but only made me that much more desperate to see the back of this forlorn community. Otherwise, what would be my fate? To take on the role of a grieving widow when Randy's name inexorably came up in that obscene lottery? Or, at a minimum, to witness the ongoing and never-ceasing deaths emanating from the mine—and know what was causing them?

I had to leave. I would go somewhere, anywhere. There was no way I could solve the town's problems on my own, or even in conjunction with the supercilious Conrad Brashear, who—I had to admit grudgingly—was in fact acting in the town's interest as best he knew how, and who himself had admitted to being perplexed at how to do any more than contain the ever-burgeoning entity growing little by little under the sod upon which we daily walked.

But then there came the earthquake.

Without warning the house began to rattle, and to my mother's dismay one of the dishes she had just washed and dried slipped out of the dishrack and fell to the floor, crashing noisily. An ominous rumbling—proceeding, it appeared, from deep underground—made every step one took, in whatever direction, something akin to walking the deck of a boat buffeted by high waves. My eyes bulging, my arms extended to maintain my balance, I cried out, "Mom! We have to get out of here!"

To my irritation, she seemed more intent on preserving the integrity of her crockery than in saving her own life. At the moment, the tremors were not so severe that they threatened to bring the house down upon our heads—but who knew how long that would last? Who was to say that this was not the beginning of a massive revolt of the earth—or of something beneath the thin layer of the earth's crust—that would result in a gargantuan cataclysm?

But just as I seized her arm and was pulling at her to leave the house, my cellphone rang.

I debated whether to ignore it and continue to shepherd my mother outdoors or to heed what has become an implacable instinct and answer the damn phone. I compromised by continuing to drag my mother through the house while seizing my purse, where the phone lay buried. I figured I might need that purse in any event, if worse came to worst and we had to abandon the house and the whole region.

The immediate area outside of the house was not itself terribly stable, and we both took a momentary refuge by slumping down on the ground and leaning up against my little car. Then I fished through my purse for the phone. I didn't have the time or the mental clarity to check the caller ID—I simply answered it.

I should have guessed it would be Conrad Brashear.

He didn't waste time on courtesies or generalities. "We have a serious problem here."

"I know that," I snapped. I couldn't even be troubled to wonder how he had gotten my number. "There's this earthquake—"

"Yes," he interrupted with equal pungency, "and I'm sure I needn't tell you what's causing it."

"No, you don't."

"Not to criticize," he said in that smarmy voice that he could seem to adopt at will, "but I'm wondering whether your tampering with the entity in the lab—"

"Hey!" I shot back. "You're not going to blame this on me!"

"I'm not blaming it on anyone. I simply don't know what's causing this. The time for recriminations is over; we all need to come together."

"And do what?" I said acidly.

Incredibly, in spite of the obvious urgency of the situation, he paused for several seconds before replying. "I think you may be able to help."

"Me?" I all but shouted into the phone. "What the fuck can I do?"

"Your knowledge of chemistry might—"

"Oh, don't give me that! You have a fleet of well-paid chemists who know a hell of a lot more about—about this thing—than I do. What do they have to say?"

He ignored that query. "Alison," he said in a surprisingly soft and gentle voice, speaking my first name for the first time, "I do think you can help. The town's fate is on the line."

"Oh, all right!" I conceded hotly, already becoming ineffably weary of this conversation. "What am I supposed to do?"

"Just stay there. I'll come by and pick you up."

All this time my mother was peering intently at me. I had a sense that she knew who my caller was, and for some reason she seemed to have a great personal stake in the upshot of the discussion. When she saw that my call was over, she said:

"What's happening? What are you going to do?"

"He's coming here to fetch me," I said, not bothering to elucidate who "he" was. "He thinks I can do something—although for the life of me I don't see what."

"You have to help the town," my mother said with a kind of whiny fervor that somehow took me aback. "What will happen if . . . ?" She couldn't finish.

"Mom, I told him I'd help—and I will."

It took only minutes for Brashear to arrive. Inevitably, he came in a comically long stretch Hummer limousine that was barely able to navigate the narrow streets of this down-at-heels district of Dunsmuir. One of the windows at the rear part of the vehicle rolled down, and Brashear did nothing but make a brief gesture of his head while some flunky leaped out and held the door open for me.

We drove off, and as Brashear pressed a lever to roll up the window, I saw my mother gazing at us with an inscrutable expression.

Inside the car, I saw two burly men along with Brashear and the driver. Their facial expressions ranged from blank to intense, and Brashear did nothing but stare at me with the deadpan expression of a cat while I tried to make myself comfortable in the lavish expanse of the limo.

Unnerved by the silence, I managed to say, "So what exactly are we going to do?"

Brashear persisted in silence, even though the rumbling and shaking of the ground was making even the expert driver struggle to maintain control as we drove off in the direction of the mine.

"I'm not sure yet," Brashear said at last.

As we passed out of the neighborhood I'd grown up in, I saw a poorly built shed on someone's property suddenly collapse in a heap. A little farther down, a garbage can suddenly rolled out onto the street directly in front of us. The driver paid no heed and ran right into it, causing it to fly crazily off into someone else's yard. There were few streetlights here, but they were all quivering like an array of unnaturally tall, thin topers about to tumble to the ground.

I somehow felt that we were heading toward the not-so-secret laboratory on the western edge of the mine, and that indeed seemed to be our destination. The limo pulled up to a large gate in the barbed-wire fence, and a quick push of a remote control caused it to open in a frustratingly slow and almost stately manner. We drove on through.

From here, I knew that the lab was to the right—but instead, we turned left.

The descending twilight made it difficult for me to piece out the terrain, which seemed starkly barren where it was not scarred with deep ruts and trenches. All of a sudden we stopped, although there seemed to be not the slightest purpose in our doing so.

Everyone except the driver began filing out of the car.

"What—what's happening?" I said in a spasm of alarm. "Where are we?"

Neither Brashear nor his two goons answered, but their emergence from the vehicle inevitably lured me out of it.

I stood as best I could on the trembling ground, trying to get my bearings. There quite literally seemed to be nothing here of any interest or relevance to our mission. But then I saw something—

And was seized by Brashear's two bodyguards.

They simultaneously held me fast and began undressing me. They seemed bewilderingly keen on not actually damaging my clothes, but in less time than it takes to tell it they had stripped me of my shoes, my blouse, my jeans, my bra, and my panties.

Conrad Brashear had the decency to turn away while I was being manhandled.

"Damn you, Brashear," I said, struggling uselessly in the grasp of the two men, "you can't—you wouldn't—"

"I'm truly sorry, Alison," he said—and, strangely enough, he sounded as if he meant it. "I really don't know what else to do."

The men carried me by my hands and feet toward what I had seen out of the corner of my eye—a kind of metal door, measuring at least five feet in circumference, fixed flat on the ground. Brashear, still doing his best not to look at my nakedness, turned a complicated series of dials in the middle of the door, then lifted the handle and tugged the heavy door open. A brief nod of his head was all it took for the men to dump me into the night-black opening that presented itself.

I fell down that hole or chute to what I assumed would be my death.

It was long—very, very long. I lost count of how many seconds, then minutes, my body slid greasily down the oiled walls of that circular passage. There was nothing I could hold on to to retard my inexorable descent into the earth, and the precipitous angle of the chute would have made it impossible for me to climb out of it even if I could somehow halt my descent.

The one thing that puzzled me—in the midst of my fury at Brashear's treachery and of my resentment at a life cut short well before it had reached its prime—was why I was not encountering the hideous creature that lay down in the depths of the mine. It was obvious that that was where Brashear had sent me, in the faint and perhaps futile hope that one more "sacrifice" might somehow halt the entity's agitation and turbulence. Was the creature at long last attempting to break out of its confines? What would it do if it did indeed emerge into the open air? What shape would it adopt when unconfined by the constricting limitations of rock and earth?

But, more to the point, why was I not perceiving its white, partially transparent, and viscous presence now?

The answer became obvious to me as I seemed to be reaching the end of the incalculably long chute. I managed to see the other end of the aperture, with a second metal door approximately like the one on the surface. But as if by some species of magic, this door suddenly opened as if it knew that a new sacrifice was heading its way.

It was only then that I plunged into the very midst of the creature.

My grotesquely tiny body melded into the heart of the thing, whose extent in every direction was utterly beyond my powers to fathom. An instinctive scream of terror was at once

muffled by the insertion of a large quantity of the entity's substance directly into my mouth and down my throat. I sensed
that, if in no other way, I would die by suffocation—not the
least merciful way to meet my end, I contemplated with a
strange sense of peace and resignation.

But the creature apparently had other things in mind. It
filled not only my nostrils and my ears, but—other orifices as
well. There was a kind of *probing* quality to the thing's otherwise unconscious-seeming entry into my vagina and my anus,
and in some baffling manner I felt that the massive, slimy folds
of the entity as they slid across my face, breasts, stomach, hips,
thighs, calves, and bottom were similarly investigative, as if it
were encountering something new to its experience.

How I continued to live while the creature was engulfing
me was something that, after my initial horror, I found myself
wondering in a state of almost impersonal rationality. I was not
in fact in any pain: I had assumed, given the loathsome death
of my father, that I would at once be burned to my bones and
then spit out; but in fact I felt virtually nothing except a kind of
mildly warm enfolding. The material I had ingested did not
seem to have done me any immediate harm, and somehow I
continued to breathe while the entity clutched me to itself.
And there was something more.

I have spoken of my sexual escapades—relatively few as
they were—during my college years. There were times when I
found the long droughts in intimacy beyond my endurance,
and so I would simply pick a man almost at random to bed
down with. For my sins, I was once persuaded—at a frat party
where everyone had drunk a bit too much—to engage in the
practice euphemistically called double penetration. The two
guys who convinced—well, let's call a spade a spade: they co-
erced—me to do this were far more drunk then I was, and in

their clumsy fumbling they failed to achieve their purpose, much to their own humiliation.

And yet, that was exactly what I was feeling now.

Yes, I had an orgasm—indeed, a seemingly endless succession of them. That might sound pleasant and desirable, even given what I knew of the creature's propensities; but the phenomenon struck me as profoundly aberrant. The realization that I was being *forced* to experience pleasure robbed the whole procedure of whatever enjoyment it might have had, even if I could somehow put out of my mind—as I couldn't—the loathsomely alien, extraterrestrial nature of the entity into whose midst I had been thrust. If I could only gain even a faint inkling of what the creature wanted from me—if, indeed, any such emotion could viably be attributed to it—then I might have been more reconciled to my presumable doom. But as the thing continued to slither across and into my body with bland inquisitiveness, I felt increasingly like some sort of bacterium that had been placed into a foreign substance by a cosmic scientist to gain an understanding of the result of the unholy experiment.

After what seemed like hours—but could in fact only have been minutes, perhaps seconds—my consciousness began to waver. I was not sure how much more of this apparently accidental sexual stimulation I could endure. Just when I seemed to be reaching my limit, a grotesque roar seemed to emerge from the depths of the creature, and I was suddenly being shot up at incalculable speed to the surface. This process took a fraction of the time I had spent in descending that greasy chute, and when I unexpectedly emerged from the creature's clutches and into the open air through a ragged gap in the earth, I could only gasp inarticulately as I landed heavily on the ground.

Only then did the cumulative trauma of my experience engender a merciful blackout.

11

As I came to, I once again found myself lying on a bed—but this time it was evident that I was in a hospital. The private room I was in was filled with the customary farrago of medical apparatus, as well as a whiteboard with cryptic abbreviated messages scribbled on it, a smallish television set mounted high on a wall, and a multi-paned window looking out on a grassy field that I recognized as part of the landscaping of the recently renovated Dunsmuir Hospital on the northern part of town.

Once I gained some clarity of vision, I saw my mother sitting in a low chair next to my bed, wringing her hands obsessively and peering up at me with a quizzical expression. As I made her aware that I was conscious, she leaped up and seemed about to embrace me, but then realized that such an act might not be good for me, so she abruptly refrained.

"Oh, Alison!" she cried, tears suddenly filling her eyes. "You're awake!"

"Yes, Mom," I said wearily, not sure she had used the correct word.

"How are you feeling?" she said anxiously.

"Fine, just fine," I said without enthusiasm—but the curious thing was that I felt exactly that. Exhausted, dazed, a bit sore, but otherwise surprisingly well.

My mother, fluttering around me nervously, now dashed out of the room, feeling the need to inform a nurse of my changed condition. Presently a crisply dressed middle-aged nurse stalked in, my mother trailing ineffectually behind, and began examining various parts of me without the slightest by-your-leave. There was, in fact, not much to examine: I assumed that much more rigorous tests had been made on me when I had first been brought in (last night, I gathered), and the nurse was now only going through the motions. I myself felt no pain, and not even any true discomfort.

The nurse was disconcertingly silent while poking and prodding me. At last I was impelled to say: "Is there anything wrong with me?"

Without glancing at my face or ceasing her probing, she said blandly, "Doesn't seem so."

"Then can I leave?" I wasn't sure I was quite up to the task, but I had no inclination to stay here any longer than necessary.

Now the nurse did look at me. "Best to stay here another night. Precautionary."

With that, the laconic creature strutted out of the room.

My mother continued to hover uselessly in the general vicinity of my bed, asking me pointless questions about whether I wished something or other. When I made an effort to get up, her eyes widened in horror, as she seemed to think it was some kind of *lèse-majesté* against hospital protocol; but as I was not connected any equipment (neither IVs nor breathing apparatus), I felt no compunction in ambling about. My backside was already aching from lying so long on my back—something I had never done for sleeping purposes—and I wanted to test the strength of my legs for purposes of locomotion.

I really did seem fine. It was absurd that the hospital wanted to keep me here another entire day, and I was tempted just to pack up my belongings—whatever and wherever they might have been—and get the hell out of here.

But before I could do that, Conrad Brashear walked in.

He probably lived only a short distance from this hospital, and who knows but that that tight-lipped nurse had at once notified him that I was once more in the land of the living? When my mother saw him enter, her jaw dropped as if she were in the presence of royalty. I almost thought she would bow or curtsy or some such thing. But he didn't give her a chance: extending a hand, her grasped hers firmly and shook it, then said:

"My dear Mrs. Mannering, how good of you to be here! But I wonder if I could have a private word with your daughter?"

The mere fact of her name passing through his lips seemed to stun her into silence, and she drifted out of the room like a sleepwalker without a backward glance.

I was in no mood to match his geniality.

"You tricked me. You tricked me and tried to kill me." I said those words with an unnatural, *sotto voce* calm that I was far from feeling.

He had the good grace to blush. "I did, Alison, and for that I apologize. I told you at the time that I didn't know what else to do, given the serious and urgent situation we were facing. And I cannot begin to tell you how glad I am that you are still alive."

"Come off it!" I shot back. "You don't give a damn about me."

"Au contraire, mademoiselle," he said with self-parodic gallantry, "but I do. You—or rather, what happened to you—has changed everything."

"What do you mean?" I said, confused.

He inclined his head in a supremely irritating gesture of patronizing concern. "I imagine your experience has prevented you from thinking clearly on the incredible nature of what you have gone through. You say I tried to kill you. And"—he gave a sudden look around the room and lowered his voice—"you are absolutely right. So why exactly are you not dead?"

The question was not rhetorical. He was gazing at me with

fierce intensity, like a college professor seeking to tease out a difficult answer out of a favored student.

He repeated the question: "Why are you not dead right now?"

My mouth dropped slowly as realization overwhelmed me. "You mean . . . like my father—like all the men who had been sent down that horrible chute, to be burned to a crisp down to their bones . . ."

"Yes, like all the *men*."

There was no mistaking the emphasis he put on that noun.

Staggered with inconceivable thoughts, I remained silent, and he went on.

"Throughout the history of this mine, virtually all those who have worked in it have been men—and, by necessity, all those who 'won' that lottery were male. Believe it or not, we have had a handful of female miners, but none of them lasted long enough to be eligible for that lottery. Women, as you know, have a bad habit of leaving employment for such escapades as marrying, having children, and so forth. All to the good of the human race, no doubt, but not helpful to the advancement of their careers in this dirty and now dying industry."

I didn't appreciate his sardonic humor, but I kept mum.

"When I—I had you consigned to that chute, I gave no thought to your gender. I will be frank in saying that my chief concern was the forlorn hope that sending a human—*any* human—down into the creature's maw would somehow cause it to retreat into itself as had happened, albeit under less spectacular conditions, in the past. And I don't deny that the thought of ridding myself of someone who had learned so many intimate secrets about the functioning of my business entered into the equation. But the result was far greater—and more beneficial—than I or anyone could have imagined."

"You mean—?" I managed to croak.

He made an expansive gesture with his arms. "You can see for yourself that the earthquake has indeed subsided. And what's more, I had my technicians conduct a somewhat crude and hasty examination of the creature—and you will be pleased to hear that it has apparently dwindled by about a quarter of its total girth. We don't have exact numbers at this early stage, but you seem to have been both good and bad for it."

Although my mouth opened, I could not utter a word.

"You see," he went on as if giving a lecture, "we don't really *know* anything about this creature. It seems absurd to think that the mere fact that a woman rather than a man gets sent down into its midst would have an appreciably different effect, but such indeed appears to be the case. Who can say why? Men and women are different, of course—biologically and psychologically. Is it something about your hormones, your brain chemistry, your, um"—he blushed again—"sexual organs that either tempted it or, conversely, repelled it? It's all a mystery. All we know is that it works. You may be the key to the future of the mine!"

His triumphant conclusion sickened and appalled me. With immense effort I said, "You can't really be serious . . ."

"Oh, but I am," he retorted. "You have emerged remarkably unscathed. True, your hair got a little singed, but that's it. I've been kept keenly aware of your condition since you were brought here last night. Trust me: the doctors have examined you with the minutest care, inside and out, and you have an incredibly clean bill of health. I wouldn't be surprised if you were actually better off now than you were before your, er, encounter with—"

"You're insane!" I shouted at the top of my lungs, rushing around the room as if looking for some means to escape. Brashear himself was all but blocking the door, and it was quite clear he wasn't going to let me out—not, at least, until he had had his say.

"Alison," he said softly, and the mere placing of my name on his tongue sent a wave of revulsion through me, "you have to understand the situation. There is now a whole new dispensation. Don't you see what has happened—and what *will* happen? You are the savior of the mine—or, at least, the people in it."

"What—what are you saying?" I said, temporizing, although I knew exactly what he was saying.

"I'm saying that there's no reason why we need to hold this dreadful lottery anymore. There is no need to sacrifice any of the men who have toiled there for so many long, arduous years. They can retire in peace and comfort—I will assure you of that. Now that we have the secret of taming the creature, of minimizing its growth, the miners can continue without the spectre of death hovering constantly over them."

"But—but that means—" I sputtered.

"Yes," he said, his voice oozing with sympathy, "it does mean that you will periodically have to—to go down that chute again. Perhaps every six months—maybe less often than that. Surely a few minutes of your time every six or eight months is worth the life of a hard-working miner."

"Oh, you evil man!" I said venomously. "Don't you try to put that kind of guilt trip on me! I'm supposed to have my body flung into that creature's clutches twice a year for—for how long? *The rest of my life?* I'm supposed to—"

"Well," he interrupted, almost chuckling while doing so, "I suspect that you can retire gracefully once you reach menopause. There really does seem something about your active sexual organs that causes the creature to react as it did. We may have to do more tests on that point."

"*Fat chance!*" I said heatedly. "I'm getting the hell out of here."

I opened a closet door, found the clothes I had been wearing the night before, and—heedless of displaying my nudity to Brashear—tossed off my hospital gown and began dressing.

"Alison," he said in a subdued voice, "I'm disappointed in you. So selfish—so little concern for others."

I wheeled on him—something not so easy to do while struggling to put my tight jeans on. "But *why me?* Why not *any* woman? Why—why not Andy Kroeber?"

I won't say that I wasn't ashamed at making such an immoral suggestion, but at this point I was desperate.

"I think you know why Andy won't serve," he said. "She is what society quaintly used to refer to as a *virgo intacta.* You know that yourself, surely."

I was long past the point of wondering how Brashear got the information he did. "Yes, I know that," I muttered.

"Now," he said almost whimsically, "I suppose you could arrange for her to be relieved of her tedious virginity, although at the moment she seems disinclined to go along. But I'll leave that up to you."

I could do nothing but level a sneer at him. "Why not some other woman of your acquaintance? Your wife, for example?"

"I'm not married," he said placidly. "It's long past the time when I should have done so and produced offspring; what with one thing or another, the opportunity has not presented itself. But there is still time."

Then a strange gleam entered his eyes. "You know, Alison, I would be happy to have you live in the comfort of my home for an indefinite period. Your services to the mine are eminently deserving of substantial recompense. And perhaps, as we become better acquainted . . ." He trailed off wistfully.

An enormous lump filled the pit of my stomach. Choking down my anger and my bile, I said shortly, "I'm leaving."

And I did.

12

But of course I didn't.

Brashear had read my character all too well. He knew I couldn't simply leave the town—and, more particularly, those poor, dirty, pathetic miners—in the lurch. I of course didn't take up Brashear's obscene suggestion of shacking up with him, with the eventual prospect of begetting his heir apparent, but I knew that my plan of stuffing my few belongings back into my Mini and heading out for the wild blue yonder would be halted by my own conscience.

Instead, I said to myself that I would stay with Mom until I could wrap my mind around this horrible, grotesque, unthinkable situation, and my own untenable position in it. I would continue to see Randy and Andy, perhaps continue to engage in physical intimacy with them. They know nothing of what had happened to me, and I will make sure they never do. And of course Mom herself is totally clueless.

That's where I am now—back in my parents' house, the house I swore I would never return to. The months have passed, but I am no closer to resolving how to get out of the quandary I have stumbled into than when this whole perplexing scenario began. Brashear actually pays me visits every now and then, in some hideous parody of courtship. But so far, I've resisted his blandishments.

The time is rapidly approaching for another encounter with the creature. I would be lying if I said I was looking forward to it—but I will say that I am ready. A few minutes of horror, and a man's life will be saved. That's a good thing, isn't it?

It is all that allows me to carry on.

www.ingramcontent.com/pod-product-compliance
Lightning Source LLC
Chambersburg PA
CBHW072005170626
46813CB00005B/2013